I0695378

BAD BLOOD

JULIE MULHERN

To the readers who've stuck with Ellison through body after body, thank you. You're the reason I write.

ACKNOWLEDGMENTS

Boy oh boy, does it take a village.
Thank you to Edie and Matt.
This wouldn't happen without you.

And, Joey, thanks for hanging with me!

I loathed Styrofoam. The oily slickness beneath my fingers. The feel of those little beads when my lips touched the rim of a cup. The SQUEAKING (infinitely more annoying than fingernails on a chalkboard). But for obvious reasons, the club didn't allow glass on the pool deck. If I wanted an iced tea (and I desperately wanted an iced tea), it was Styrofoam or nothing.

"May I please have a Tab in the can?"

"Sure thing, Mrs. Russell?"

"Jones."

"Sorry about that, Mrs. Jones." The boy behind the snack bar looked harried. With only a few days until Labor Day, the pool was crowded with families eager to enjoy the last precious moments of summer. That meant the snack bar, which smelled of equal parts French fries and chlorine, was equally crowded.

"No, thank you." I accepted the already-sweating, hot pink can and stepped outside, lowering my sunglasses from the top of my head to the bridge of my nose.

"Ellison!"

I turned and spotted Jessica Hendrick. "Jessica, how nice to see you. How was Michigan?" Jessica and her family spent most of July and August in Saugatuck.

She kissed the air near my cheek. "Wonderful. It's always wonderful, but it's good to be home. *So* good to see you! I heard you had an eventful summer."

I'd found a few bodies. Why anyone bothered calling that eventful was beyond me. After all, I found bodies year-round. I'd given up on being shocked. But I couldn't say that. "I suppose I have. Say, that's a cute suit."

Jessica, who wore a brown swimsuit covered with orange and white daisies, rested her hand on her hip. "Thank you. I swear, finding a flattering suit gets harder with each passing year."

"You're right about that." I wore last year's black tank with a matching sarong.

"Now that I'm back, let's get together for lunch."

"I'd like that." I nodded toward the other side of the pool, where Libba lounged on a chaise while guarding mine. "I'll call you, and we can set something up for after the holiday."

"Perfect. Talk soon."

I skirted the edge of the water as small children with bare feet practiced that I'm-hopping-fast-not-running-so-the-life-guards-can't-scold-me gait unique to sunbaked pool decks. A couple of teenage boys played gutter ball. At the diving well, a little girl with dripping pigtails and a frilly pink bathing suit yelled, "Momma, watch me!"

A woman left off smearing zinc oxide across a little boy's nose and called, "I'm watching."

Sure that she had her mother's attention, the little girl leaped off the end of the high dive, the embodiment of four-year-old bravery. She catapulted through the air in silence.

Anticipating her triumphant smile, I waited for her to break the surface.

And waited.

Her mother, who'd gone back to covering her son in white goo, didn't seem to notice that her daughter might be in danger.

I took a step toward the water's edge, ready to dive in.

But before I had the chance to kick off my flip-flops, the lifeguard, a young woman with blonde hair and a deep tan, jumped from her chair into the pool. The resulting splash garnered attention, and the child's mother finally realized something was wrong. She rushed to the edge of the pool as the guard kicked deeper under the water.

I stood frozen, holding my breath, until the lifeguard surfaced with the child.

"Suzie!" The mother lifted the crying girl from the lifeguard's arms.

Suzie, who was still coughing up water, buried her head against her mother's chest and sobbed.

The lifeguard hauled herself out of the pool and crouched next to Suzie and her mother.

I recognized the lifeguard. Her parents lived on the next block over, and years ago, she'd babysat for Grace. Paula? Patricia? Pam! "Well done," I told her as I tried to remember where she was in college.

She gave me a brief nod, her attention on Suzie.

I left them, took my seat next to Libba, loosened my sarong, and stretched out my legs on the chaise.

"What's that all about?" She waved toward the concerned circle around Suzie and her mother.

"Do you remember Pam Brewster—the girl who used to babysit Grace?"

She tilted her head and stared at me, the mirrored lenses of her sunglasses reflecting my face back at me. "Why would I remember one of Grace's babysitters?"

"Point taken." A hot breeze ruffled my hair, and I brushed a loose strand behind my ear. "Her parents are Sonia and Fred Brewster."

"Again—who?" Libba went so far as to lower her glasses so she could gaze at me over the rims. The expression in her eyes was not impressed.

"They live in our neighborhood. Fred makes flanges."

"Come again?"

"Flanges. Something to do with plumbing. Fred developed a better flange. When Henry was alive, he said Fred could buy and sell most of the people we know." Which was Henry's way of saying Fred was filthy rich. "At any rate, his daughter Pam just saved a little girl."

"How old is the girl?"

"I'd say around four."

"No, Ellison. Pam Brewster."

I did some quick math. "She's around twenty. Maybe twenty-one. KU. She goes to KU."

Libba's face twisted with distaste.

"What?" There was nothing wrong with the University of Kansas. Plenty of fine people attended.

"Prudence is walking toward us."

I glanced over my shoulder.

Unfortunately, Libba was right. Prudence Davies was marching toward us. The woman was horrible. She had horse teeth, a mean streak, and the emotional intelligence of a rock. I would have disliked her even if she *hadn't* had an affair with my late husband—although *affair* was too genteel a word to describe their relationship.

"What do you want, Prudence?" Even lounging, Libba managed to look down her nose.

Prudence pulled her thin lips back from her horse teeth and glared at me as she clutched a Styrofoam cup. "I wasn't asked to serve on the committee for the philharmonic ball."

Why was she telling me? "That's too bad."

"I'm told it's your doing."

"I don't have that kind of power." But Mother did. And she

disliked Prudence as much as I did. I'd have to ask her if she was behind this latest snub.

"I don't believe you." Her cup squeaked, and I barely concealed a shudder. If she recognized my weakness, she'd be squeaking like mad.

Instead, I managed a polite smile. "Believe it or not, I don't spend my days pondering ways to make your life unpleasant. If you want to work on the committee, I suggest you take it up with the chairman. I'm sure she'd be happy to have another volunteer."

The sneer on Prudence's face deepened. We both knew my suggestion would make her appear desperate. "You think you're so—"

"Go away, Prudence," Libba sounded bored. "Don't you have some half-blind married man to seduce?"

A sly, satisfied expression flashed across Prudence's long face.

"She already has," I murmured. "Another one?"

Libba took off her glasses, the better to scowl at Prudence. "What is it with you and adultery?"

"You're one to talk," Prudence bit back.

Libba shook her head. "Charlie was divorced before we got together."

"Well, Fob is going to divorce his wife." Her voice was strident.

"For you?" The words slipped out. Unkind. Mainly because they were true. No man in his right mind would leave his wife for Prudence. Also, what was Fob short for? Father of the bride? Free on board? Full of booze? If he was dating Prudence, the latter was probably right.

Prudence's cheeks flushed an unbecoming red. "You're not any better than the rest of us, Ellison Russell."

"Jones," I corrected. Why did no one get that right?

She growled. "You're an average painter who got lucky. You

don't have any real talent. This—" she pointed at Libba "—slut is your only true friend. You married a cop because no man of substance would take you. You—"

She'd insulted my career, my best friend, and my husband in less than twenty seconds. "Enough. You're a horrible woman. Mean. Spiteful. Petty. I hope this Fob comes to his senses and sees you for what you are, a horse-toothed harpy with the morals of a tomcat."

"I know Henry's secrets. You'd better hope I don't share them."

Libba snorted. "At this point, every soul in this town knows that Henry had a thing for kinky sex."

Did she have to be so loud? My gaze traveled across the pool. Suzie and her mother were forgotten. Everyone was staring at us. Heck, even Pam, the heroic lifeguard, was gaping at us. I guessed that Prudence and I had been equally loud. My heart stuttered, and I said a silent prayer of thanks that Grace was at Peggy's and not here at the pool. She'd hear about this, but at least she didn't have to hear it for herself.

"He had other secrets." Prudence smirked at me. Dear Lord, she was even louder than Libba.

Henry's other secret was equally sordid. My late husband had enjoyed blackmailing people. A sin I hadn't discovered until after he died. Had Prudence discovered that secret? Was she *threatening* me? "I didn't have anything to do with the committee selection for the ball. But I can assure you, I'll be making my opinion known."

"You'll tell her to ask me?" Prudence's smug smile rubbed me the exact wrong way.

I shook my head. "I'll tell her she's better off without you."

Prudence threw her drink at me.

I spluttered as soda pop splashed across my face and chest. I jumped to my feet, making windshield wiper motions across my breasts. "Have you lost your mind?"

"Don't mess with me, Ellison."

"Or what?"

Prudence's complexion darkened to a brickish hue. If she had a second drink, I'd be wearing that one, too. "I'm warning you—"

"You're warning me? If I were you, Prudence, I wouldn't threaten me again."

Her lips curled away from her teeth. "Planning on finding my body?"

"It wouldn't make me sad." I stepped toward her.

"What are you doing?" She held up her hands and retreated a step as if I meant her actual harm. "Stay away!"

So. Much. Drama. I rolled my eyes, pulled off my soda-dotted sunglasses and shook them, splattering the pavement with additional droplets. "You assaulted me."

"I'm a witness," said Libba helpfully.

Rivulets of sugary liquid ran down my arms and between my breasts. "I'm going to the locker room for a quick shower."

Prudence planted her hands on her hips. "We're not done talking."

"I beg to differ."

"The philharmonic, Ellison. Fix it."

"I'm not remotely involved with this year's ball. And I will not be fixing your problems." I took a step toward the locker room.

Prudence grabbed my arm, and I froze. We both stared at the place where her fingers circled my sticky forearm.

"Release me."

Being Prudence, she ignored my demand. Instead, she shook my arm. "I mean it, Ellison. I can make things unpleasant for you."

I wrenched my arm free. "Go to hell, Prudence."

With the eyes of half the pool upon me, I lifted my chin and walked to the locker room as if I wasn't covered in cola. As if

Prudence and I hadn't provided a week's worth of grist for the gossip mill. As if having my late husband's infidelities tossed (literally) in my face didn't bother me in the least.

I stepped into the club's rudimentary locker room. The place smelled of chlorine and mold and whatever cleanser the staff used to combat the mold. Leaving my flip-flops on, I took the fastest shower of my life.

I lifted my chin even higher on my way back to my lounge chair.

When I arrived, Libba offered me a wry smile. "She's a witch."

"I can come up with a better word."

"Ha. I can too. Do you think she's really found another marriage to ruin?"

I remembered the brazenly sly expression that had flashed across Prudence's face. "I'm afraid so."

"What secret could Henry have? He's been gone for more than a year."

"No idea," I lied. I'd told only one person about Henry's vile actions. One. And bound by attorney-client privilege, he would never, ever tell another soul.

"She was probably making it up to get under your skin."

"Probably," I agreed. I let my gaze study the club members clustered around the pool. No one glanced our way. No one. It was as if they were embarrassed that they'd been caught staring during Prudence's meltdown. That embarrassment wouldn't keep them off the phone later. Mother would hear about this. And fast.

Hopefully, whoever called Mother would tell her that I'd behaved with decorum befitting a Walford. As for Prudence, Mother would make it her mission to ensure she never served on a worthwhile committee again.

My Tab was no longer cold, but I took a sip anyway. "What were we talking about before Prudence interrupted?"

"Grace's babysitter. Frankly, we needed a different topic."

She shook a copy of *Vogue* with Lauren Hutton on the cover at me. "Berets. They're showing berets. Do they imagine we're Mary Tyler Moore tossing hats into the sky? Since when are berets symbols of female empowerment?"

"Not a fan?" I kept my voice mild, not wanting to incite further comment. Libba was passionate about style, and berets quite obviously didn't pass muster.

"And the clothes? Loose, drapey, long. Apparently, we'll all be wearing potato sacks this fall." Libba favored a more revealing style.

"A travesty."

She lowered her chin and glared at me over the rims of her glasses. "I had your back with Prudence."

"True. My apologies. Obviously, we'll be ignoring everything in the latest issue."

"There's an interesting article about whether or not you need a psychiatrist."

"Me personally?"

She huffed a brief laugh. "Not you. You roll with the punches."

"I might have a touch of neurosis."

"You don't. You should. If I found bodies the way you do, I'd be a blithering mess. You just keep going."

"Don't say that like it's a bad thing."

"My point is you're ridiculously well-adjusted."

"Thank you. I think." There were days—the days I found bodies—when I wanted to run home, curl into a ball, and scream into my pillow. I never did. Mother might bemoan my finding bodies; but she hadn't raised a woman who hid beneath the covers. I faced my problems. Well, most of them. Henry's blackmail was locked away and best forgotten. And I hated that Prudence had made me remember those innocuous-looking files.

"What time are you meeting with Courtland?" Libba glanced at her watch.

"Not until tomorrow morning. Eight o'clock." I was working with the assistant club manager on the end-of-summer pool party scheduled for the Sunday of Labor Day weekend. "We're just reviewing details."

"What are you doing tonight?"

"We're going out to dinner. Stroud's." My husband adored their fried chicken.

"When does Aggie get back?"

Our housekeeper, Aggie, had taken some time off to go to the lake with her boyfriend. Since no one appreciated my cooking, we'd been eating out. A lot.

"Can't be soon enough." I relied on Aggie more than I realized. Her absence was a challenge.

Libba nodded. "With your cooking, it's a wonder you haven't killed someone."

I shot her a withering look (she wasn't the only one who could gaze over the rims of sunglasses). "I haven't put my mind to it. Yet."

CHAPTER TWO

nne Everist and I sat across from Courtland Gerhardt in his small office. So small that our knees hit the edge of a desk cluttered with sample napkins (bittersweet, sage, and bark—presumably for an autumnal event), four styles of glass vases, stacks of invoices, and sample menus.

I didn't hold the clutter against him—the man was busy. And seldom in his office.

It was just after eight-thirty. We'd been at this for thirty minutes, and we were making no progress.

Anne was a woman without enough to do. Sadly, that meant she dived into details. Obsessed over them. Would the napkins exactly match the flowers? Would both buffets (one for children and one for adults) be doubled-sided? And the menus? We needed to review them. For the fourth time. The children would eat hot dogs, hamburgers, corn on the cob, baked beans, and macaroni and cheese. Anne wanted to add a vegetable medley and salad. I was ready to strangle her.

If Courtland was losing his patience, he hid it well.

I was less sanguine. Discreetly, I checked my watch.

"Should I call for more coffee?" asked Courtland.

"Please. As for the buffet, unless their parents are fixing their plates, the kids won't touch the healthy options."

Anne pursed her thin lips and patted her teased hair. She was far too young for a helmet. Someone should tell her. It wouldn't be me. Then, she offered me a tight smile. "You're underestimating their palates."

I was not. The teenage girls would go through the adult buffet, selecting salad, grilled chicken or salmon, and roasted vegetables. The children and the teenage boys would scarf dogs and burgers and macaroni like there was no tomorrow. "The menu is set. We're not changing it now."

Courtland offered me the smallest of smiles. How he put up with us all was beyond me. Then again, the man was ridiculously good at his job. "There isn't any available space on the kids' buffet."

"Then we cut something. Do they really need tater tots?"

Yes, they did. The kids might revolt without them. I took a sip of coffee and offered Anne an olive branch. "If their parents want them to eat vegetables, they can serve them from the adult buffet."

"Ellison, we're not offering a single healthy item."

"Corn on the cob is healthy." Ish. It would be swimming in butter and salt, but it was still a vegetable. Or was corn a grain? How did I not know the answer? "It's a party. Let the kids indulge."

Anne shook her head, and not a single hair on her head dared move. Then she smoothed the unwrinkled fabric of her bright green Lilly skirt. "What kind of example are we—"

"I'm sorry to interrupt." A middle-aged man wearing a traumatized expression and a greenskeeper's uniform stood just outside Courtland's door.

"What is it, Bill?" Did I see relief flash in Courtland's hazel eyes?

Bill wrung his hands. "We have a problem."

Courtland leaned back in his chair as if he expected nothing less. "Oh?"

Bill's eyes were wide. Blown. The poor man had been traumatized. "On the golf course. Sand trap. Seventeenth hole."

We all waited for more, but Bill was too busy staring a hole through the carpet to tell us.

"What's the problem?" Courtland prompted.

Bill raked his fingers through his hair. "There's a body."

Courtland stiffened. "A member?"

Bill dragged his palm across his mouth as Courtland rested his forearms on his desk.

We all waited.

"I don't know if she's a member," Bill finally replied. "But she's been shot."

One of the glass vases on Courtland's desk fell to the floor, shattering.

Anne shrieked.

I swallowed a sigh and reached for the phone. "I'd better call Anarchy."

Courtland shoved the phone toward me, and I pushed a button for an outside line and called my husband.

"Jones." Anarchy sounded tired. The phone had rung shortly after nine last night, and he'd left to investigate a homicide. When I'd left for the club this morning, he still hadn't come home.

"It's me. How's your case?"

"We arrested the husband about an hour ago." He sighed. "Did you find a body?"

"I did not." I glanced at the man in the doorway. He was pale beneath his tan, and his hands were shaking. "Bill found the body."

It was easy to imagine Anarchy closing his eyes, leaning his head against the back of his worn desk chair, wishing for a reprieve before he had to deal with another murder. He'd be well within his rights to snap at me. Instead, he asked, "Where are you?"

"The club. The body is in the bunker on the seventeenth hole."

"Who?"

"A woman. She's been shot."

"I'm on my way."

I hung up the phone.

"What do we do?" asked Bill.

"My husband is on his way."

Bill frowned at me. "She's dead. A doctor can't help her."

"My husband isn't a doctor. He's a homicide detective."

"You're the one!"

Oh goodie, I was famous. "As for what you can do, make sure no one else goes near the body."

"We have golfers on the course."

"Tell them to skip the seventeenth hole."

He blinked. "They won't like that."

Just wait till the police closed the course as a crime scene. "They'll get over it."

Courtland stood. "I should probably go out there. May I assume the party plans are finalized?"

Anne opened her mouth as if she intended to again lobby for vegetables.

I spoke, "They're finalized."

"But—"

"Anne, Courtland has bigger problems than putting salad on a kids' buffet. Drop it."

She pressed her hand against her chest as if I'd mortally wounded her. "Well, I—"

"It's one night." I used the placating tone I usually saved exclusively for Mother. "One night."

"Fine," she huffed. "But I want fruit on the dessert buffet."

I glanced at Courtland, and he gave a tiny nod.

"Done." As if any card-carrying kid would pick melon balls over an ice cream sundae or Bomb Pop.

Courtland waited until Anne and I exited his office, then he closed the door and locked it. "Thank you for all your work on the party. I'm sure everyone will love it." He gave us a final nod, then trotted after Bill.

"Who do you suppose it is?" asked Anne. "On seventeen, I mean. A member?"

Random people didn't wander onto private golf courses and get murdered. Dread settled in my stomach, turning the coffee already there into acid.

"Should we go out there?" she asked. "We might be able to identify the body."

Ghoulish curiosity never ceased to amaze me. "It's a crime scene, and Courtland's already there. If it's a member, he can identify her."

She stared at me, and I couldn't help but notice a tiny clump in her mascara.

"We might disturb evidence," I added.

"What if it's not a member? Someone Courtland doesn't recognize?"

"Then the police will identify the body."

She lifted plucked brows. "I must say, given your history, I thought you'd be more engaged. They might need us."

"Someone is dead, Anne. They might be a friend."

Anne nodded eagerly. "Exactly. And we can help catch her killer." Her curiosity wasn't merely ghoulish; it was ghastly.

"By tromping through the crime scene?"

"By identifying the body in a timely manner."

"For the next few hours, the police will be collecting evidence, not searching for suspects."

Anne huffed her displeasure as if I were personally respon-sible for ruining her fun. "What are you going to do?"

"Go home."

"That's it? Won't the police want to interview us?"

"Were you on the golf course last night or this morning?"

"No," she admitted grudgingly.

"Neither was I. I doubt either of us have anything to contribute." I dug my keys out of my handbag and walked toward the parking lot.

Twenty minutes later, I sat at the kitchen island and stared at Mr. Coffee's sunny gingham face. "Another body."

You're worried about your mother's reaction.

"It won't make her happy."

It's not as if you found the body.

I waved my hand. "Details." Details that would not make a whit of difference to Mother. I groaned. "What if it's someone we know?" At the highly disturbing rate at which my friends and acquaintances were dying, I'd soon have none left.

Don't kids sneak onto the golf course to drink and make out?

"The greensman said 'woman,' not 'girl.'"

Brnng, brnng.

I stood and reached for the receiver. "Jones' residence."

"Ellison, it's your mother."

Mr. Coffee groaned on my behalf.

"Good morning, Mother."

"You had an argument with Prudence Davies at the pool."

"Yes."

"And now she's dead. Murdered."

"What?" I pressed my palm to my rapidly pounding heart. "The body on the golf course belongs to Prudence? How do you know?"

"I have my sources. Hunter Tafft is on his way to your house as we speak." Hunter was a lawyer. The lawyer. The one who kept Henry's secret. He'd also represented me when I was last suspected of murder.

"Why?"

"Don't be stupid, Ellison. You had a fight with the woman yesterday afternoon, and this morning she's dead."

"I'm sure lots of people wanted to murder Prudence."

"Be that as it may. You publicly argued. I heard she retreated from you as if she feared for her safety."

"She threw a soda in my face. That is hardly motive for murder."

"She threatened to reveal Henry's secrets." Mother paused, and it was all too easy to picture her with pursed lips and narrowed eyes. "Does he have any secrets I haven't already heard?"

"Henry's secrets died with him." Almost the truth.

"Apparently not. Not if Prudence was threatening you with them. Do not talk to the police without Hunter present."

"I'm married to the investigating officer."

Mother sighed as if I were being deliberately obtuse. "Do you really believe they will let him investigate Prudence's murder? His wife is a suspect. Heck, he may be an accomplice."

"We had nothing to do with her death."

"I believe you, dear. Now convince the police and everyone we know. Because, until you do, you're guilty."

Ding, dong.

Saved by the bell. "Someone's at the door."

"Hopefully, Hunter. Remember, don't talk to the police unless he's with you."

With shaking hands, I hung up the phone and followed the dogs into the front hall. Max's stubby tail was wagging a mile a minute. Finn, the Airedale we took in with Beau, danced on his paws. Whoever was on the stoop was a friend.

I plastered on a smile and opened the door.

Hunter Tafft had silver hair, a perpetual tan, and a smile that made most women go weak in the knees. He flashed the smile at me.

My knees remained strong.

"Your mother called."

I nodded as Max jammed his nose into Hunter's crotch. I grabbed my dog's collar and dragged him away. "She's worried that I'm suspect number one in Prudence's murder." I tried to make Mother's worries sound silly.

The look on Hunter's face said I had failed. "So she said."

I opened the door wider. "You'd better come in. Coffee?"

"Please."

"Have a seat in the living room."

"That's not necessary." He followed me into the kitchen and pulled out a stool.

"Cream or sugar?"

"Black."

I poured him a cup and slid it across the island. "So, what do we do?"

"Tell me about your argument with Prudence."

"She blamed me because she wasn't asked to be on a committee for the philharmonic ball. I told her I didn't have that kind of influence."

His gaze over the top of his mug said he wasn't buying that for a minute.

I held up my hands. "I was not responsible."

"Then what happened?"

"She threw her soda in my face and threatened to spill Henry's secrets."

"Did she know?" He'd asked the most important question. Had Prudence known Henry was a blackmailer?

"She was probably making up something to get under my skin." Mission accomplished. I'd stared at the ceiling until the wee hours waiting for Anarchy and worrying about what Prudence knew. "I'm sorry Mother insisted that you make a house call. She overreacted."

"I don't mind. Do you want to review what you'll tell the police?"

"The truth. I had nothing to do with Prudence's death."

"Pretend I'm a police detective." His pleasant demeanor disappeared, and he stared at me with a gimlet eye. "You fought with the deceased."

"Argued," I corrected as I tucked a strand of hair behind my ear.

"About?"

"Her exclusion from a volunteer position."

"She held you responsible?"

"She did."

"Are you responsible?"

"No." The truth would set me free.

"Then why did you argue?"

"She didn't believe me. She threatened me."

"How? With what?"

"My late husband was…kinky. She threatened to tell people."

Hunter tapped his chin with the tip of elegant index finger. "Hardly news, Mrs. Jones. What was the real secret?"

Hunter had a point. I did need to consider how I framed the truth. I stared into my coffee cup.

The back door flew open, and Anarchy strode into the kitchen.

I lifted my head, and our gazes met. His tired eyes widened when he saw Hunter sitting next to me.

"Mother sent him." I offered Hunter a grateful smile. "Not that you aren't always welcome."

"I'm glad you're here, Tafft." Anarchy rubbed the back of his neck as tension seemed to radiate from his shoulders. "Detective Morrison would like to speak to Ellison at the station."

My grip on my coffee mug tightened. "Why?"

New lines seemed to be etched into my husband's lean face. "How long has it been since you laid eyes on your gun?"

A chill traveled from the top of my head to my toes, tightening every muscle in my back. Painfully. "Why do you ask?"

"Your gun was found in the sand trap."

"That's impossible."

"I wish." He shook his head, and his gaze slid away from mine. "I'm off the case, and you're a suspect."

"That's ridiculous. I didn't kill Prudence."

"I believe you."

"Then why on earth do I have to go to the station?"

"The kids spent the night with friends last night, and I got called out on a case, so you were alone. You don't have an alibi. You argued with the deceased in front of witnesses. And it appears that your gun was used to commit murder."

I clutched the edge of the island as the blood drained from my face. "How do you know it's my gun?"

"Monogrammed grip. EWR."

I shook my head. "That's not possible."

Anarchy wrapped me in his arms, but he held me stiffly. "I found the gun. I identified it."

My stomach churned. "This can't be happening."

Anarchy's answering expression was grim.

Hunter rose from his stool. "I'll drive you to the station."

Anarchy released me, moving toward Mr. Coffee and pouring himself a cup. "The detective, Danny Morrison, is old school. Not one of my fans."

"You're coming with me." It wasn't a question.

His lips thinned. "I can't. Besides, they're getting a warrant to search the house. Someone should be here."

I closed my eyes and took a deep breath, hoping to tamp down my rising panic. "I need you there."

"They might suspend my badge."

"I need to make a call." Hunter's gaze bounced between us. "May I use the study?"

"Of course."

He stepped into the hallway, leaving me with Anarchy. "You have to come with me. Please." Walking into the police station without my husband's support wasn't something I could handle.

The expression in his eyes was pained. "The captain ordered me to stay away."

A chasm—dark, swirling, hopeless—had opened beneath my feet. I crouched and scratched behind Max's silky ears. He nudged me, and when I didn't smile at his antics (I didn't have it in me), he gave me a rare lick. I wrapped my arms around his doggy neck and stifled the urge to cry. "Please don't make me do this without you."

Anarchy gave a brief nod. "I'll come. But they won't let me in the interrogation room."

"That's why I'll be there." Hunter had returned. His presence was reassuring. "Let's get going."

Anarchy took a sip of coffee. "I'll follow you."

"What?" Anarchy wasn't driving with me? What if we got separated in traffic? What if…there were too many what ifs to count.

"You need time to talk to your lawyer. Whatever you say to him is privileged."

"And what I say to my husband?"

"I'm a cop, Ellison."

The chasm beneath me opened wider.

CHAPTER THREE

The hum from the fluorescent bulbs grew louder, becoming an obnoxious buzz. Then the bulbs flickered, and the hum lessened. Whenever the lights flickered, my left eye twitched. Hunter and I had been sitting in the harsh, unflattering glare for thirty minutes. And I knew to expect another flicker in—I glanced at my watch—three minutes and twenty seconds.

Hunter seemed unperturbed. His posture was perfect. As was his silvery hair. If the fluorescent lighting bothered him, he didn't show it.

He hadn't even wrinkled his nose when we were led to this tiny room. He'd ignored the lingering aroma of stale cigarettes, industrial cleanser, burnt coffee, and desperation.

He'd hardly noticed the tired metal chairs and single scarred table.

Meanwhile, my throat felt raw with unspent emotion, and a headache was building behind my left eye.

Hunter nodded at the mirror that hung across from us, leaning close enough to whisper in my ear. "They're watching. Waiting. Hoping to unsettle you."

"Mission accomplished."

He flashed me a brief grin. "You have nothing to worry about."

Easy for him to say. I lifted my brows. "You sure about that?"

"I promise."

My shoulders relaxed infinitesimally.

The door opened, and a detective I'd never met stepped into the small room. His face was fleshy. His nose was red. And his eyes were mean. He stared at me for a long second, then his lip curled. I'd been found lacking.

I sat straighter. He didn't impress me either. The detective's gut hung over the edge of his belt, a stain marred his shirt, and he had the air of a man who was counting the moments until cocktail hour. Canadian Mist. Neat.

"Ellison Jones." He had a two-pack-a-day voice.

"Yes."

"I'm Detective Morrison."

"Nice to meet you, detective."

"Hmph." He lowered himself into the chair across from me and opened a file. "We have questions."

I nodded and tried to read upside down. Prudence was barely cold. How had they filled a file so quickly?

Hunter tapped my foot with the tip of his polished wingtip, and I lifted my gaze from the detective's file.

Morrison steepled his fingers and glared at me.

I glanced at Hunter. Was Morrison for real? Did he expect me to fill the silence with a tearful confession?

"Your questions, detective?" Hunter was too polite by far.

"You felt the need to bring a lawyer?"

I sat straighter in my uncomfortable chair. "That is my right."

"Tell me about Prudence Davies."

"What about her, detective?"

"How long have you known her?"

"Years. Decades. I can't remember when I didn't know Prudence." A sudden wave of sadness washed over me. I hadn't liked her—okay, I'd actively disliked her—but I hadn't wanted her dead.

"You didn't like her." It wasn't a question.

I folded my hands in my lap and kept my mouth shut.

"Well?"

I tilted my head.

"Did you like her?"

"I did not." The pain behind my left eye sharpened.

"Why not?"

"She was not a likable woman."

"She had an affair with your late husband?"

"Yes."

"How did you feel about that?"

"When I found out about it, I wasn't happy."

"I bet."

"Water under the bridge. I moved on."

"You argued with Ms. Davies yesterday?"

"I did."

"About?"

"She blamed me for excluding her from a charity committee."

"Did you?"

"No."

"Then why did she blame you?"

"It was easier for her to blame me than accept the truth."

"What truth?"

"People didn't like her."

"You didn't like her."

"We covered that, detective," said Hunter.

Morrison scowled at Hunter before turning his irritated expression on me. "Ms. Davies threw a drink in your face."

"She did."

"She threatened to reveal your late husband's secrets."

"My late husband was a philanderer with…interesting proclivities. That's been an open secret since his death."

"Maybe he had other secrets."

I forced a shrug. "Maybe he did, but I'm not aware of them."

"Where were you last night?"

"At home."

"Can anyone verify that?"

"My husband was with me until about nine o'clock. He got called out on a case. After that, I was alone."

He clicked his pen and made a note in the file. "No alibi. You were at the country club when the body was discovered." He leaned in, covering the file with his bulk and taking up half the table.

"I was. I called Anarchy."

"But you left." He made leaving a crime scene an accusation.

"I did."

"Why?"

"I didn't want to be in the way."

"Most people who brush up against a murder case stick around to see what happens. They're curious. They want to know who's dead."

I wasn't most people. I discovered bodies. Often. Too often. After a body was found, there were hours upon hours of evidence collection and photography. Important work. But watching it was about as exciting as watching paint dry. "Not me."

"Hmph. You know your gun was found at the scene?"

I rubbed my left temple. "So I've been told."

"Any idea how your gun turned up at a murder scene?"

"None."

"When was the last time you saw it?"

I'd been asking myself that exact question. Endlessly. "I don't remember. I keep it in a drawer in my bedside table."

"You have children at home?"

"I do."

"And you don't keep your gun in a safe?" He made me sound like a terrible mother.

"They're not small. And we've discussed gun safety. Neither of them would touch the weapons in the house."

"Weapons? Plural?"

"Anarchy has firearms."

His cheeks flushed slightly, as if he'd forgotten I was married to one of his colleagues. "Who knew where you kept your gun?"

"Anarchy. The kids. Maybe Libba."

"Libba?"

"My best friend."

"I'll need her information."

"Of course, detective," Hunter replied.

Morrison leaned back in his chair, laced his hands over his paunch, and gazed at me. "Here's how I see it. We have a dead woman you didn't like. Heck, she carried on with your late husband. They embarrassed you. Badly. From what I've heard, she's been a thorn in your side ever since. Yesterday she threatened you. Publicly. Then, she turned up dead in a sand trap. At your country club. Shot with your gun."

He didn't know that for sure. I'd often listened to Anarchy bemoan the delay in getting ballistics reports. There was no way Morrison had results on bullets for a shooting less than twenty-four hours old. My disbelief must have shown on my face because his expression darkened.

"I'm married to a homicide detective. I know a thing or two about catching killers. I promise you, if I were going to kill someone, I wouldn't leave my monogrammed gun at the crime scene."

"You panicked."

"I didn't kill her."

"You don't have an alibi."

"I didn't kill her." It bore repeating.

He smirked as if he'd beaten me at a game I didn't know I was playing. "You'll get your chance to prove that. I'm arresting you for the murder of Prudence Davies. You have the right to remain silent. Anything you say can and will be used against you in a court of law. You have the right to talk to a lawyer for advice before we ask you any questions. You have the right to have a lawyer with you during questioning. If you cannot afford a lawyer, one will be appointed for you before any questioning if you wish. If you decide to answer questions now without a lawyer present, you have the right to stop answering at any time. Do you understand these rights?"

"You're arresting me?" I didn't have *time* to get arrested. The kids were days away from going back to school. I had paintings that needed finishing. Aggie was out of town. And the dogs needed daily walks. I turned toward Hunter as the blood in my veins turned to ice.

"We'll get you out," he promised.

"The kids—"

"Anarchy will take care of them."

"The dogs—"

"Anarchy will walk them."

"The—"

"Anarchy will handle it." Hunter turned toward Morrison. "I'd like a moment with my client."

With poor grace, Morrison gave us the room.

Hunter grabbed my cold hands, squeezing tightly. "They're going to take you to jail. Whatever you do, do not talk about your case. Not to anyone. I mean it, Ellison. Not a word."

Jail? "But—"

"We'll get a bail hearing set within a few hours. You'll be granted bail. You'll be home for dinner. Now, what did I tell you?"

"Don't talk to anyone about my case." The words came out

in a monotone. There was an exceptionally good chance I was in shock. There was an equally good chance my headache might kill me.

"We'll get this figured out."

"He believes I killed Prudence."

"And Anarchy and I know you didn't."

"Mother…" She was going to string me up by my toenails.

"Frances will probably have Morrison's badge over this. When push comes to shove, she's in your corner."

Push had definitely come to shove.

"She'll be so outraged that someone has accused her daughter of murder, she won't have the bandwidth to be mad at you."

He was trying to cheer me up, but he was seriously underestimating Mother. She could be furious with multiple people at once. Rather than argue a moot point, I nodded and did my best not to cry.

"Don't worry, Ellison. We'll get this worked out."

Don't worry? Easy to say when you weren't the one arrested for murder.

THE CLANG OF THE CELL DOOR ECHOED THROUGH MY BONES, AND I ground the heels of my hands into my eyes. How had this happened? One moment I was chatting to Mr. Coffee, Mother's reaction to the body on the golf course was my biggest worry, and now, a few hours later, I was in jail for murder. Panic tightened my throat, and I squeezed back tears.

"You okay?"

I wasn't alone. I dropped my hands and stared at the young woman on the cot across from the cell's door. She had dark curly hair tied back with a faded bandana and wore cut-off denim overalls over a tie-dye T-shirt. Her knees were drawn up to her chin, and she was idly picking at a loose thread on her overalls. Mascara smudged the skin beneath her eyes. Tired. Tough. Not the sort of woman I met for bridge at the club.

"Are you okay?" she asked again. Her voice was surprisingly soft.

"Not really." I was in JAIL, and, while I wasn't paying attention, someone (Detective Morrison) had slipped an icepick into my brain.

Her expression softened, and she scooched to the far side of the cot. "Do you want to sit?"

"That's kind of you." A flutter of gratitude stirred within me, and I joined her on the rock-hard cot.

"What are you in for?" The woman's eyes were sharp. Intelligent. Curious.

I swallowed my dread. "Murder." The word tasted bitter on my tongue.

Her eyes widened. "Wow. And I thought I was in trouble." She let out a low whistle.

I closed my eyes and tried to ignore the vague smell of urine and cigarettes that seemed to seep from the walls. "What did you do?"

"I took a baseball bat to my boss's Mercedes."

That was worth opening my eyes.

She grinned, revealing a slight gap in her front teeth. I was reminded of Lauren Hutton. My cellmate was just as pretty.

"Why?"

She pulled at another thread, ripping it free. "His wife found out about us, and he fired me." Her voice, which had been light, tightened with an edge of deep-seated resentment.

"You were sleeping with him?" I sounded awfully self-righteous for a woman in for murder. A flush of heat crept up my neck. She'd been kind, and I'd insulted her.

"I didn't set out to screw the boss. He's handsome for an older guy. He flirted with me. Touched my shoulder when he walked by my desk. Tucked a lock of hair behind my ear when I brought his coffee. Flowers appeared on my desk. Then he stole a kiss by the copy machine and told me he thought about me all the time. The next thing you know, we're taking long lunches." She waggled her brows in case I missed her innuendo. "At first it was a thrill— having an older, successful man want me—but I started to lose sleep. He was married. I'm not *that* girl, or at least I didn't think I was. The guilt ate at me. When I tried to end things, he told me if I broke things off, I'd be fired." She chuckled, but there was no humor in it. "I guess he did that, anyway. He said I'd violated the company's morals clause. Well, he violated it right along with me. But I'm the one who'll have a two-year gap on my resumé. How do I explain that when I apply for my next job?"

How would she explain a conviction for malicious vandalism? No one would be eager to hire a woman who'd pulverized her last employer's car with a baseball bat.

I kept that thought to myself. "I didn't mean to sound…" my voice trailed off. Judgmental. I hadn't meant to sound judgmental. "My late husband wasn't…faithful."

Darla waved a dismissive hand. "Don't sweat it. Most people get judgy. I figure we've all got our stories, right?" She destroyed another thread on her overalls, then looked up, her sharp eyes studying me. "So, murder, huh? That's heavy."

Hunter's warning rang in my ears. "I didn't do it," I whispered. For some reason, it seemed important that she believed me. "I find bodies. Sometimes." Often. "I've never killed anyone."

"Bodies? Wow. I just find trouble." She folded over her legs, stretching and moaning softly. "They don't make it comfortable in here. And you, you seem... like you're not used to roughing it."

"I'm not," I admitted, a lump forming in my throat. "This is a nightmare."

"Yeah, well, the good thing about nightmares—eventually you wake up." She patted my leg, and her kindness made my jaw ache with the need to cry. "I'm Darla, by the way. Darla Higgins."

"Ellison Jones."

She held out her hand, and we shook. "So, who are you supposed to have killed?" Her eyes were bright with interest.

Not. A. Word. To anyone. That's what Hunter had told me. "I'd rather not talk about it." I crossed my arms over my chest and rubbed. It wasn't cold in the cell, but I felt chilled. "Tell me, how did it feel to swing that bat?"

Darla grinned again. "Fan-freakin'-tastic. The sound of that headlight shattering was the sweetest thing I've ever heard. Right up until I swung that Slugger down on his hood. Who knew crunching metal sounds better than Elvis?"

"Remind me not to get on your bad side."

Her grin widened. "He had it coming."

"No argument." Her married employer had seduced her and then fired her for violating a morals clause. Shame on him. He'd gotten off easy with a damaged car.

"He's claiming I'm a threat to him and his family. Wants me to rot in here. I'm not a threat. I worked all my anger out on his car. He loved that Mercedes even more than he loves his wife. I'm not sure he even likes her." Another thread broke beneath her fingers. If she kept pulling them, she'd soon be naked. "I didn't expect him to fire me. Not for her."

Had she had feelings for him? Feelings he'd trampled. "I'm sorry."

Darla shook her head. "It wasn't some grand romance. Besides, I'm free now." She glanced around our cell and chuckled again. "I guess I should say I'm free of him."

"Are you good with numbers?" I could help her.

Darla frowned at me. "What do you mean?"

"Are you good with numbers?" How much clearer could I be?

"I was working as his bookkeeper."

"Would you be interested in a job at a bank?"

She nodded slowly. "Are you offering?"

"I am."

Her eyes widened. "Just like that?"

"Just like that."

"You realize I have an issue with my temper?"

"I got that. When you get out of here, look me up. I'll have a job waiting for you."

CHAPTER FOUR

The courtroom wasn't as grim as the jail cell, but it still hummed with a tense, low energy that tightened every muscle in my shoulders and spine. I tried to concentrate on the sunlight filtering through tall, arched windows and the dust motes dancing in the air.

Tried and failed. My thoughts were too tangled. My emotions were too raw.

I'd been charged with murder. Me. Ellison Russell Jones.

I glanced over my shoulder, but the seats behind me remained resolutely empty. My husband wasn't here. He hadn't come. His absence, and my terror, had me gripping the edge of the defendant's table until my knuckles whitened.

Hunter leaned in. "Deep breaths, Ellison. This is a formality. You'll be home soon." He squeezed my arm lightly, his calm demeanor a stark contrast to the chaos raging inside me. I wanted desperately to believe him, but the phantom clang of the metal door at the jail still echoed in my mind. He'd explained what would happen. This was a pre-arraignment bail hearing. I didn't have to enter a plea. Hunter would argue that I should be released on my own recognizance. Failing that, bail would be set.

I glanced down at my lap, where embroidered ladybugs marched across my navy wrap skirt. Ladybugs and a scoop neck T-shirt. I still wore what I'd put on to meet with Courtland. Hardly appropriate for court. I swallowed a hysterical giggle and peeked over my shoulder again.

My heart skipped a beat when the door swung open and sank when a man I didn't know strode toward us. He carried a leather briefcase and wore a sharp suit (not as sharp as Hunter's, but still sharp). Slicked-back hair revealed a high forehead and cut cheekbones.

"Who's that?" I whispered.

"The assistant prosecutor," Hunter replied. "His name is Jim Steele."

Oh. Him. Jim Steele. The man who would accuse me of murder in an open courtroom. When he reached the prosecutor's table, he smiled at me.

I read enough naked ambition in that smile to make my skin crawl. Jim Steele wanted to make a name for himself by putting me in prison.

"All rise," said the bailiff. "The Circuit Court of Jackson County, the Honorable William Caldwell presiding, is now in session."

I stood on shaky legs and watched as Judge Caldwell took his place behind his bench.

"Please be seated."

I sat (my knees gave out) and glanced at Hunter. Judge Caldwell and Daddy were rivals on the golf course, vying for bragging rights every other Sunday. My stomach clenched tighter. Did their rivalry help me, or did Judge Caldwell hold a grudge? Did my future depend on whether Daddy had beaten him last week?

"It's fine." Hunter patted my hand.

Was it? Not from where I sat.

The prosecutor stood. "Your Honor, the State requests a moment before proceedings." He paused, letting his gaze sweep over me – taking in my country club attire – before settling back on Judge Caldwell. "Given the high-profile nature of this case, and your connection to the defendant's father, the State feels it is prudent to request that Your Honor consider recusing himself. No one wants any appearance of impropriety, however unintentional."

My breath hitched.

Judge Caldwell scowled down from his bench. I'd never seen a stonier expression (as Frances Walford's daughter, that was saying something). "My acquaintance with the defendant's father will in no way affect my impartiality."

"Understood, Your Honor." The prosecutor looked pale, and he tugged at his collar as if it were suddenly too tight.

I hoped it choked him.

"Proceed," said the judge.

Steele launched into his arguments, detailing the public altercation at the pool, the threats, my handgun at the crime scene, and my lack of an alibi. He made Prudence sound like a saint (nothing was further from the truth) and made me out to be a vengeful harpy—one who still harbored murderous anger over Henry's infidelity. He used words like "flight risk" and "danger to the community."

The blood slowly drained from my face, leaving me cold and lightheaded. This was really happening. And the prosecutor spoke well. Convincingly. Heck, I was half-persuaded I'd done it, and I knew I was innocent.

When Hunter's turn came, he was direct and concise. A spat on the pool deck did not equal a motive for murder. Why would I care about my late husband's secrets? I'd moved on. Remarried. Then he spoke about my family's long-standing history in Kansas City, my husband's job as a homicide detective with an impressive clearance rate, my career as a successful artist, and the sheer absurdity of my murdering anyone. He concluded by saying I'd cooperate fully with the investigation and then asked that I be released without posting bail.

Jim Steele stood. "Your honor, the defendant is charged with murder." He sounded furious.

"The defendant is innocent until proven guilty," the judge replied.

I needed to talk to Daddy about letting Judge Caldwell win their next eighteen. I crossed my fingers and waited.

"Given the circumstances," Judge Caldwell's voice echoed in the quiet courtroom, "the court finds that Mrs. Jones does not pose an immediate flight risk, nor is she a danger to the community."

I drew my first full breath in hours. The dread that had been a physical weight on my chest suddenly lifted, replaced by a surge of pure, unadulterated relief.

"She is released on her own recognizance."

The prosecutor's mouth puckered as if he'd sucked a lemon.

I threw my arms around Hunter and hugged him.

Only when I pulled away did I see them. Anarchy. Karma. And Mother.

Mother's expression was one of barely concealed disapproval. And I had to face her. Suddenly, returning to jail didn't sound so bad.

Hunter and I stood and made our way toward my family.

"This is an all-time low, Ellison." Mother seethed, as if I'd gotten arrested just to annoy her.

"Frances, that's hardly fair," said Karma. "Ellison is innocent. She'll be exonerated."

I flashed my half-sister a grateful smile.

Mother side-eyed Judge Caldwell's bench. "Murder follows Ellison like a dog on a leash. People talk. And mark my words, they're talking now."

"Let them," said Anarchy.

Mother turned toward him, her expression cold enough to freeze the blood in a lesser man's veins.

"I mean it." Anarchy doubled down. "Let them talk. Ellison didn't kill Prudence. The police will find the real killer."

"Will they?" Mother shook her head. "They've already made an arrest. Why would they investigate anyone else?"

She wasn't wrong. That's what terrified me most of all.

"Then I'll investigate." Exactly what he'd been told not to do. It would put his job at risk.

Grateful tears welled in my eyes. My freedom mattered more to him than the job he'd always wanted.

"Ellison?" Anarchy stepped forward and wrapped me in his arms.

It had been a terrible, awful, no-good day, and his arms felt like home. I melted into his embrace and buried my face against his chest.

"Ellison!" Mother's horror at our public display was evident in her outraged tone.

Reluctantly, I lifted my head. But rather than address Mother, I stared into my husband's coffee-brown eyes. "Would you take me home, please?"

"Of course." He brushed a kiss across my forehead, and we both ignored Mother's displeased exhalation.

"Wait." I turned toward Hunter. "I'd like you to represent my cellmate. I'll pay for it."

His perfect brows lifted. Mother's carefully plucked brows lifted even higher.

I ignored Mother, focusing on Hunter. "You'll like her."

"Innocent?" he asked mildly.

"Guilty."

Hunter's brows lifted all the way to the middle of his forehead. Mother's touched her hairline.

"She took a baseball bat to her boss's car."

"Ellison!" Mother was utterly scandalized.

I waved off her disapproval. "There were extenuating circumstances. I'm certain her boss would prefer to avoid a public trial."

Hunter nodded as if I'd explained every sordid detail. "I see. Her name?"

"Darla Higgins."

"Darla?" Mother practically shrieked, no longer able to contain her chagrin. "You befriended someone named Darla? In jail. Really, Ellison, have you lost your mind?"

"She's a lovely young woman. I offered her a job at the bank."

Luckily, there was a chair behind Mother because she swayed and collapsed. "Why are you doing this to me?"

"Helping someone in need?" I asked sweetly.

"Consorting with a convicted criminal."

"She hasn't been convicted."

"Yet."

I glanced at Hunter. "I have a feeling Hunter will be able to get all charges dropped."

"Hunter needs to focus on your case!"

"I want to go home." Curling up in my husband's arms with an overfilled wine glass sounded like the only sanctuary left to me.

Anarchy's arm tightened around my waist. "As you wish."

"Don't you have the Hallowells' party tonight?" Leave it to Mother to ask an unwelcome question.

"Harper will understand if we miss it."

"No." Mother wagged her index finger at me. "You're going."

"Mother—"

"Ellison Walford Russell—"

"Jones," I corrected without any real heat.

"You are going to put on a new dress from Swanson's, lift your chin in the air, don a carefree smile, and go to that party. Show everyone there that this—" she wrinkled her nose at my recent incarceration and pending charges "—is utterly ridiculous."

"I'm sure Ellison is exhausted." Karma's sympathetic eyes told me she'd guessed my plans for the couch and a bottomless glass of wine.

"Too bad," Mother replied. "She's going. They're going. I don't care if I have to drag her there myself. You will face this down, Ellison."

"Fine." I sounded petulant (more like a teenage girl than an adult woman), and I couldn't muster the will to care.

A few minutes later, Anarchy opened his car's passenger door, waited until I sank into the seat, and then slid behind the wheel. He didn't slide the key into the ignition. Instead, he stared through the windshield.

I followed his gaze.

He'd parked in a surface lot, and the only thing in front of us was the faded-brick facade of a turn-of-the-century building.

Given the late afternoon heat, sitting in a closed car without the air conditioning running was just shy of crazy. "What's wrong?"

His fingers, already on the wheel, flexed before gripping more tightly.

"Anarchy?"

He didn't look at me. "I'm sorry."

The pain behind my left eye lessened. "For?"

"You shouldn't have had to ask me to accompany you to the station. I should have been in the courtroom before you arrived." Finally, his head turned, and I clearly saw the tortured expression in his eyes. "I'm an idiot."

I shrugged, minimizing the hurt I'd felt. "Henry wouldn't have come at all."

"Henry was a bad person and a worse husband. Doing marginally better is hardly a badge of honor."

"Your captain told you to steer clear." I understood. Sort of.

"You're my wife. Our marriage is more important than my job."

"I'm sorry I put you in this position."

"You didn't. This is on whoever killed Prudence." His lips thinned. "Can you forgive me?"

"Already forgiven. Already forgotten."

He loosened his death grip on the steering wheel and reached for my hand. "I love you, Ellison Jones."

At least one person could get my name right. "I love you, too. Now—" I blinked back a haze of tears "—would you please take me home?"

He gave my fingers a gentle squeeze before starting the car and pulling out of the parking space.

I adjusted the air-conditioning vent until it blew onto my chest. "Is Mother right? Will the police look for other suspects?"

The storm in his brown eyes gave me my answer.

I leaned my head back and groaned. "There must be at least a dozen people who wanted her dead."

Anarchy turned south on Broadway. "How many of those people had access to your gun?"

Someone had snuck into our home, gone through my things, and stolen my gun. What if the kids had been home? They'd killed Prudence. Would they have hurt Grace or Beau? My blood ran cold. "It's terrifying to think about."

He gave a grim nod. "Who knew you kept a gun in the bedside table?"

"You. Mother and Daddy. Libba. The kids—"
"Libba?"

I shook my head. "Libba didn't steal my gun. What's more, she had no reason to kill Prudence."

He grunted. Not arguing but not agreeing.

"The kids may have mentioned my gun to their friends."

"And?"

"Let's assume Grace mentioned where I kept my gun to her girlfriends. If one of the girls told their parents…" I frowned. Was this the right track?

"If one of them told their parents?"

"My gun could easily become cocktail party chatter." I pitched my voice higher.

"Poor Ellison. She's found another body."

"If I were her, I'd be afraid to leave the house."

"Bless her heart, she does keep a gun in her nightstand."

A glimmer of a smile skated across Anarchy's lips. "I see what you mean. But the killer still had to get into the house."

"How often do we neglect to lock the doors?" With the four of us (five counting Aggie) going in and out all day long, the kitchen door was seldom locked.

"You're right. We need to be more careful. Also, if anyone could get in, we're back to looking at who wanted her dead."

I swallowed. "How did Prudence die?" I knew she'd been shot, but there was a difference between a close-range shot to the back of the head and a bullet in the stomach.

"She took a bullet in the chest."

"On the golf course?"

"It looked that way. There was a lot of blood."

"What was she doing there? Why would a grown woman be on a golf course at night?"

"Why would anyone be on a golf course at night?"

"Kids have been sneaking onto the golf course to drink beer or canoodle since I was a girl."

His lips quirked. "Canoodle?"

"Canoodle."

"Did you sneak onto the golf course?"

"I may have."

"Interesting. With whom?"

"No one important," I replied airily.

"But you canoodled?"

"Marjorie was the canoodler in our family." And my sister's favorite canoodling partners were usually my boyfriends.

"Hmm. Maybe I can change your mind about that."

"I'll canoodle with you anytime."

"I can pull over."

"We're almost home."

"Your point?"

"It's more comfortable to canoodle on a couch than in a car."

"You speak from experience?"

"I plead the Fifth."

Grace and Beau met me at the front door. Almost tackled me at the front door. Their arms surrounded me, and I pulled them close. The dogs danced around us, excited by the high emotion and group hug.

"We were so worried," Grace scolded.

That made three of us. "Hunter took care of it."

"So, it's over? You've been acquitted?"

"Not exactly."

My daughter's eyes narrowed in a fair approximation of Mother's favorite expression—

irritated exasperation. "Then it's not taken care of."

"I've been released on my own recognizance."

"What does that mean?" Worry creased Beau's tanned brow, and shadows lurked in his eyes. Finn leaned against Beau's legs and whined softly.

"It means the judge thinks Ellison is innocent." Anarchy had followed me into the house. He sounded confident, as if the pending murder charge was a mere blip.

"Why did they arrest you at all?" Grace demanded.

"Have either of you mentioned my gun to any of your friends?"

Beau shook his head, and I couldn't resist smoothing his blond hair back into place.

Grace paled.

"Sweetheart?" I asked softly.

"Last week. Or the week before that." She squeezed her eyes shut, and long seconds passed before she admitted, "I honestly can't remember."

"How does something like that come up?" asked Anarchy.

A deep flush colored her cheeks, and she shook her head.

"You can tell us, honey."

Her mouth opened, but she didn't produce any words.

"It's important, Grace." Anarchy's tone brooked no argument.

Grace gave a small, pained nod. "Kim was looking for a nail file and checked her mom's nightstand. She found—" she pressed her hand against her mouth and stared at the floor as if she wished it would swallow her whole.

"What did she find?"

"A sex toy," she whispered.

Oh, good Lord.

"I said that the only interesting thing you kept in your drawer was a gun."

"Who was with you?" asked Anarchy.

"Peggy, Debbie, and Kim."

If one of those girls had told their mothers, the location of my gun might have easily come up at a cocktail party, or bridge table, or luncheon. I suppressed a groan. There were too many suspects. How would we ever narrow the field?

CHAPTER FIVE

Harper Hallowell was a lovely woman. Pretty. Stylish. Smart. And it was a wonder her husband put up with her. Harper's hobby was houses. She and Phillip moved every two or three years. Harper would find a dated house with good bones, completely redo it, live in it for six months, then search for her next project.

Her latest project was a 1930s, Spanish-inspired, five-bedroom home with an odd-shaped Talavera-tiled pool that took up much of the backyard. Her décor leaned heavily on the house's Spanish influences. The dark hue of the ceiling beams was reflected in the mahogany-toned leather couches, jewel-toned carpets, and heavy wooden furniture.

Anarchy and I passed through the house in search of the bar. "I wonder if she stored her furniture," I whispered as I took in an ornate armoire stained the color of burnt coffee.

"This isn't usual?"

"This is a set piece. She'll be sick of it in three months." We reached the doors that opened to the backyard and stepped outside. I leaned against the loggia's wall, the stucco rough and warm against my bare arms. The soft glow of wrought-iron lanterns dispelled the surrounding shadows. The air, thick with the humidity of Kansas City in August, was redolent with the scents of jasmine and the rich aroma of grilling chorizo. Potted ferns, heavy and dark green, filled the corners, and emotional notes from a flamenco guitar wafted from the living room. The air-conditioning wafted too. This spot on the patio was the best of both worlds; the coolness of the house married with the magic of a perfect summer evening.

Anarchy reached out and fingered a lock of my hair before brushing the back of his hand against my cheek. "Growing up, half my friends lived in houses that looked like this." He was from California, not Missouri.

For a moment, I got lost in his eyes. We were a quiet island in a sea of well-liquored guests.

He leaned down and pressed a soft kiss against my cheek. "You okay?" he murmured, his breath warm against my skin.

"I will be." What we had was everything, far too precious to be derailed by a murder charge. Besides, I was innocent. That had to count for something.

His eyes held mine, a silent conversation passing between us. He loved me. I loved him. Nothing, especially not Prudence's death, would change that.

"Ellison, I'm so glad you joined us tonight. What do you think?"

I dragged my gaze away from Anarchy and focused on our hostess.

Harper waved an elegant hand at her beautiful patio.

"It's gorgeous," I replied honestly.

"What about you, Anarchy?" She offered him a warm smile. "Do you like it?"

"Very nice." He jerked his head toward a sideboard in the living room. "I noticed you have an impressive collection of Santos figurines."

I followed his gaze to a grouping of creepy wooden statues,

but Harper seemed delighted by Anarchy's comment. "Thank you. I found the first one, Mary holding the baby Jesus, at an antique store in San Diego, and I was hooked. The rest required multiple trips to Mexico."

"She's Our Lady of Guadalupe."

Harper tilted her head. "Pardon?"

"The statue you bought in San Diego. She's Our Lady of Guadalupe, the patroness of Mexico."

"You're very knowledgeable." Harper didn't sound entirely thrilled.

"I grew up in California. Big Spanish colonial influence."

"Of course. Well, if you're interested, the bar is set up in Phillip's study. Through there." She pointed toward an arched entrance. "The sangria is marvelous." She took a few steps and then turned back to us. "You must meet Piper's son. Let me introduce you. Chuck," she called to a man standing by himself, "come meet the Joneses."

"Who's Piper?" Anarchy whispered as a tall young man with a receding hairline and superior expression walked toward us. His nose was so high in the air, he was in danger of drowning in a rainstorm.

"Harper's sister," I whispered back. "She lives in Bucks County."

"Ellison, Anarchy, meet my nephew, Chuck Corrigan, from Pennsylvania. Chuck, these are the Joneses. Ellison is the artist I was telling you about." With the bare-bones introduction made, Harper disappeared into the crowd.

Chuck extended his right hand as if I were lucky to touch him. "Pleased to meet you." His fingers were damp, and his handshake was limp. When he released me, I resisted wiping my palm on my dress.

Instead, I asked, "What brings you to Kansas City, Chuck?"

"A job." He let the words hang a beat too long before

swirling the drink he held in his left hand. The ice cubes clinked against the glass.

He couldn't be more forthcoming? He wanted me to ask. I grudgingly played along. "Oh, really? What are you doing?"

"I'm a law clerk." He lifted the drink to his lips and took a sip. The rim of the glass didn't hide his satisfied smile.

Anarchy shifted, and I sensed his sudden tension. "Which court?" he asked.

"The Sixteenth Circuit Court." Chuck made it sound like he'd been appointed ambassador to the Court of St. James.

My husband visibly stiffened.

"What do you do, Anarchy?" Chuck inquired, tone pitched somewhere between idle curiosity and faint amusement.

I wasn't sure I bought Chuck's ignorant act. If Harper had told him about me, she was sure to have mentioned that I was married to a cop.

"I'm a homicide detective."

"Is that so?" Chuck could give Mother lessons on sounding condescending.

"Where did you go to law school?" I deftly redirected the conversation.

"Harvard." Chuck took smug complacency to a new level.

In my experience, people who attended Harvard, especially Harvard Law, mentioned their alma mater at every opportunity. That might fly on the East Coast. Not so much in the Midwest. Especially when coupled with a superiority complex. Someone needed to tell him how his conceit might harm his career.

Anarchy's hand pressed against the small of my back with unexpected urgency. "It was a pleasure to meet you, Chuck. If you'll excuse us, I promised my wife a sangria."

Chuck offered a regal nod, as if we'd been dismissed.

Anarchy hurried me across the room.

"What's your rush? You know I don't actually drink sangria."

"Were you or were you not considering telling that man that he has a bad attitude?"

"Maybe." For his own good. And the satisfaction of taking him down a peg.

"Not a great idea. Not when he's going to be clerking for the court where you'll be charged with murder."

I stopped dead in my tracks as the air whooshed from my lungs. "What?"

His hand slid around my waist. "Let's get you a drink."

"Let's get me two."

"Ellison?"

I turned and forced a smile. "Jinx. Don't you look gorgeous!"

My friend, who wore a coral-hued silk kaftan that set off her deep tan, frowned at me. "We need to talk. Now. Anarchy, do you mind?"

He stared at her for long seconds before offering a brief nod. "Of course not. Ellison, I'll find you with that drink."

"This way." Jinx led me onto a brick pathway that skirted the pool. She didn't stop until we reached a secluded bench over-looking the far side of the dark water. I watched as the lights from the house shimmered on the pool's surface—gold, silver, turquoise. Jinx sat, and when I didn't immediately join her, she grabbed my arm and pulled me down. Only when we were both seated did she fix her sharp gaze on me and demand, "Spill."

My shoulders sagged. "You heard?"

"I'm surprised no one else knows yet."

"Me too. Obviously, I didn't kill her."

"Obviously. Who did?"

"No idea. At the club, when we had our tiff, she admitted to an affair. She said he was going to divorce his wife for her."

Jinx snorted her disbelief.

"Does the name Fob mean anything to you?"

"No." She tapped her lips with her index finger. "Do you think this Fob's wife killed Prudence?"

I wished the solution was that neat. That easy. All wrapped up in a tidy bow. The only problem was that I'd never heard of anyone named Fob. How would his wife know to sneak into my house and steal my gun? "I don't suppose you've heard anyone discussing where I keep my gun?"

She frowned. "I have not."

That was bad news. If I told the police that the gun's location had been openly discussed, they might have to expand their investigation. "I'm afraid the detective running the case has stopped looking for other suspects."

She patted my knee. "You've got the department's best detective in your corner. The two of you can figure this out. I'll help."

I leaned forward and gave my friend a quick hug. Jinx's assistance would be invaluable. There was little that happened in our crowd that she didn't hear about. She collected gossip like a numismatist collected rare coins. And she was just as jealous about protecting her collection. "Thank you."

"Fob, huh?" Jinx, who wasn't a hugger, extricated herself from my arms.

"Fob."

"Something to do with a pocket watch?"

"I have no idea." I waved off a mosquito.

"Prudence and Jessica Hendrick spent a lot of time together before Jessica left for Michigan. You should ask her."

Really? I tried to wrap my head around Jessica and Prudence as friends. "I thought Jessica had better sense."

"Jessica is too nice for her own good. She felt sorry for old horse-teeth."

There were much worse things that could be said about Prudence. Still... "We shouldn't speak ill of the dead."

Jinx's eyes sparkled in the light reflecting off the pool. "Why ever not?"

Because it would come back to bite me. Of that, I was sure.

"Have you been hiding in the shadows?" Libba was clearly

peeved. She crossed her arms over her chest, tilted her chin, lifted her left eyebrow, and looked down at our bench. Her body language said it all—I needed to face these people with a confident smile.

"Jinx and I took a moment to chat."

"Chat later. Tonight, act like you've got the world by the tail on a downhill pull."

I didn't want to.

"She's right," said Jinx. "Besides, half the party is whispering about Prudence. If you listen, you may hear something useful."

With a reluctant sigh, I stood and plastered a smile on my tired face.

Anarchy found me as I was entering the living room, pressing a glass of white wine into my hand. "Sorry it took so long. Perry's here." Our friend Perry was a raconteur, and his stories were seldom short.

I took a sip of buttery Chardonnay and replied, "My friends insist that I mingle like I don't have a care in the world."

"Not the worst advice."

"Doesn't it make me look callous?"

"It's no secret you didn't like her." His gaze flickered over the chattering crowd, assessing. "No one here did."

"Jinx suggested we eavesdrop."

"Jinx is a smart woman. Divide and conquer?" He glanced at his watch. "Meet you back here in thirty?"

Not for a second did I think Anarchy would hear anything useful. People tended to either clam up or nervously blabber around homicide detectives. Was I being pessimistic? He might find a nugget in the blabber. And pigs might fly. I gave a reluctant nod, and he kissed my cheek before melting into the crowd.

I did not want to do this. Give me a root canal, give me another hour with Detective Morrison, give me a week on Mother's bad side. They were all better than listening in on my friends' conversations.

I retreated to a secluded alcove off the living room, drawn to the floor-to-ceiling windows with their view of the pool. The lights were low enough for me to see outside. Liz and Perry were chatting with Robbie Smart. Charlie Ardmore had his arms around Libba's waist. She stared into his eyes. A faint smile touched her lips, and her brows lifted just enough to give her an air of quiet vulnerability, as though she were offering Charlie a glimpse into her heart.

I inched behind the curtain, blocking the ambient light. I'd never seen that expression on my best friend's face, and I wanted to commit it to memory. If I could paint her looking like that, I'd have the perfect gift for their wedding (if she ever told him *yes*).

"Are you crazy?" The voice was so low I wasn't sure I actually heard it. But it came from the other side of the curtain. If I shifted, they'd find me.

Someone had joined me in the alcove.

"She's dead. We're safe. You don't need to worry." A man replied.

"She could've told—"

"She didn't." Flat. Final. Absolutely certain.

"You can't be sure." The whisperer sounded panicked.

"I can."

This—exactly this—was what Jinx had hoped I'd hear. My neck prickled as I slowly turned, still hidden by Harper's heavy drapes.

Had Prudence been blackmailing the man? Had he killed her?

A crash from the living room shattered the air—broken glass, the unhappy exclamations of people who'd been splashed or startled. I jerked away from the sound.

The brief second of hesitation cost me. When I pulled the

curtain aside, I was alone except for the lingering scent of Paco Rabanne Pour Homme. When I hurried into the hallway, all I saw was a man's back vanishing into the crowd in the living room.

CHAPTER SIX

I t wasn't until I was safely buckled into the passenger seat of Anarchy's car that I recounted the conversation I'd overheard in the alcove.

Anarchy rubbed his chin before starting the engine, both actions slow and considered. "You didn't see who it was?"

The car's headlights swept the street still crowded with other guests' automobiles.

"No."

He drove to the corner before asking, "A man and a woman?"

"I assume…" I bit my lower lip and wished for the umpteenth time that I'd managed to get a glimpse of the people who'd joined me in the alcove. The frustration was real. I'd overheard a suspicious conversation and had nothing but hearsay to show for it.

"But?"

I squeezed my eyes shut as if the streetlights were a distraction. "The drapes muffled their voices. I could barely hear the whisperer. I honestly couldn't tell if they were a man or a woman." I'd strained to hear the words, not the speaker's sex.

"Anything else?"

"The man wore Paco Rabanne Pour Homme."

"Half the men in your circle wear that cologne."

Not Anarchy. When my husband wore cologne, he wore Aramis. If he knew how the combined scents of leather and oakmoss and *him* made my knees go weak, he might wear it more often.

"Most men don't wear enough cologne for the scent to linger behind them." I laced my fingers in my lap. Short of asking Harper for the guest list and tracking down and sniffing every man who attended, we were at a dead end. "Did you learn anything?"

His eyes were hidden in the shadows, but I noticed the small smile on his lips. "Do you know someone named Nancy Fleetwood?"

"We've met." Different country clubs, different schools for our children—we'd crossed paths at parties and galas.

"Apparently Prudence did something to wreck Nancy's relationship with a guy named Hatton English." He shifted his gaze to me and shook his head. "Where does your set come up with these names?"

"Pot. Kettle. Black."

"Fair enough. But Hatton English?"

Hatton, I knew. Middle-aged before his time. He was slightly paunchy, somewhat stuffy, and very smart. "Give a child a name to live up to. No one named Hatton English will grow up to be a garbage collector or ditch digger."

"No, he's probably a lawyer or a money manager." No flies on Anarchy.

"And when someone hears your name for the first time?"

He winced. "If they don't realize I'm a cop, they assume I lead Zen retreats. Or deal weed."

Nothing could be further off base. Anarchy was the

straightest arrow I'd ever met. "Hatton is a money manager. Boring, except for his ability to provide good returns. He's immensely proud of those returns. Immensely proud."

He nodded. Vindicated. "Speaking of pride, let's talk about Chuck. There's no chance of keeping the arraignment from your friends. Not with Chuck as the clerk."

My lungs deflated. "Isn't there some kind of attorney-client privilege?"

"That's between you and Hunter. As long as Chuck doesn't disclose private court business, he's free to discuss a public arraignment with anyone. Including his Aunt Harper."

And his aunt could discuss it with everyone in Jackson and Johnson Counties. Not that I blamed her. I was the woman who found bodies, not the woman who killed people. The murder charge would be big news. And Harper had an inside man.

I swallowed a groan. "Any idea when the arraignment will take place?"

"That's a question for Hunter."

We drove a quiet block before I said, "Jinx suggested I talk to Jessica Hendrick. She spent a lot of time with Prudence before leaving for Michigan."

"How well do you know Jessica?"

"Reasonably well. She suggested we get together for coffee on the day Prudence accosted me at the pool. Why?"

"We do not want to give the impression that we're interfering with Morrison's investigation."

"Morrison isn't investigating. He's sure I'm guilty."

His left hand stayed steady at ten o'clock, but he slid his right across the seat and squeezed my fingers. His hand was warm and comforting, and his touch was enough to give me a glimmer of hope. Enough to loosen the tight knot in my chest. Together we'd caught numerous killers. This would be no different.

"Jessica may know whether Prudence has made anyone incandescently angry recently."

"Okay." He turned onto our street, and the streetlights traced bars of gold across his face. "Have you ever been hypnotized?"

"Never. Why?"

"It might help you remember when you'd last seen your gun."

I had friends who'd used hypnosis to try to quit smoking. None of them had found it terribly effective. But with Anarchy looking at me the way he was, I'd try anything.

He pulled into our driveway and put the car in park.

"I'll give it a try." My doubts bled into my voice.

"It's the gun that's the problem, Ellison. There's no getting around Prudence being shot with your weapon."

"Were there any other prints on the gun?"

"The report isn't back yet. If I had to guess, I'd say that's why you haven't been charged yet."

I groaned; the sound reflected my frustration.

"Hey, now." His fingers brushed along my jaw, a warm whisper against my skin. "I'll solve this. I promise."

I wanted nothing more than to curl up in a ball and let him fix this mess. But I wasn't the kind of woman who let a man solve her problems. We were in this together. "Back to Nancy and Hatton. Did you hear what Prudence did?"

"No." He opened the driver's side door. "Maybe Jinx knows."

"If Jinx knew, she'd have told me." Instead, she'd told me to visit with Jessica.

Anarchy closed his door, circled to mine, and opened it, offering me his hand.

I took his fingers and stood.

He gently brushed a strand of loose hair away from my face. "You look very pretty. I should have told you earlier. And what you did—going to that party with your head held high—that was brave."

I took a tiny step forward, resting my forehead against the hard plane of his chest. "I didn't feel brave." My voice was disturbingly small.

"Ellison..."

I lifted my head.

Anarchy's gaze lingered on me, searching, as though he could read my every worry. His thumb traced the curve of my jaw, feather-light, sending a shiver all the way to my toes. His hand cradled my cheek, and I melted into his strength, leaned into the steady calm that always anchored me. His lips met mine in a tender, unhurried kiss. My fingers curled around the lapels of his jacket, holding on until the world blurred to nothing but us. We were in this mess together.

And if Mother learned we'd been making out in the driveway, we'd be in a bigger mess.

I pulled away, my lips tingling.

"Where are you're going?"

"Inside."

"When you open that door, the dogs will need you. Grace will need you. Beau will need you."

"And?"

He pulled me flush against his chest. "What if I need you?"

"I'll be quick."

He stole another kiss, warm and quick and full of promise. "I'll hold you to that."

"You take care of the dogs. I'll take care of the kids."

"It's a deal."

DID *DID YOU HAVE A GOOD TIME LAST NIGHT?*

I closed my fingers around Mr. Coffee's pot. "The party was very lovely."

That doesn't answer my question. Mr. Coffee winked at me. Winked!

A blush warmed my skin, and I lifted my cup to my lips to block my too-observant coffeemaker's view of my pink cheeks. "Jinx thinks I should call Jessica Hendrick."

Still avoiding the question? When had Mr. Coffee become so sassy?

I got enough sass from Grace, and, frankly, it was too early in the morning for me to be teased by my coffeemaker. "I don't suppose you noticed anyone sneaking into the house."

I wish I could help. Mr. Coffee sounded sincere.

So sincere, I forgave him the teasing. "Don't worry about it. I don't know what I'd do without you."

Brnng, brnng.

I glanced at the clock. Too early for a social phone call. That meant Hunter or Mother. I crossed my fingers for the former and picked up the receiver. "Jones' residence."

"Ellison Russell—"

"It's Jones, Mother."

"Fine. Ellison Jones. You were seen kissing in your front driveway. You have a perfectly good house. What were you thinking?"

"I was thinking that I'm scared, and I needed a moment of comfort."

"So badly you couldn't walk the fifteen feet to the front door."

"Exactly."

There was a beat of silence. Mother hadn't expected me to agree. She recovered quickly. "Don't be ridiculous. You didn't kill that dreadful woman. You'll be exonerated."

"The police are convinced they've caught the killer."

"I called Jimmy." My "Uncle" Jimmy was a police commissioner. "They are now pursuing other suspects."

"Did you discuss this with Hunter before you made the call?"

"Hunter is your lawyer, not mine." That was a "no."

"And you don't think it will antagonize the investigating detective to have my family go over his head?"

"What's your point, Ellison?"

"Everyone is telling me to tread lightly." I didn't add that she'd trampled into the investigation with all the subtlety of a herd of rampaging rhinos. "That goes for all of us."

She sniffed, "Well, if you don't want my help."

"I want your help." Sort of. "But let's work as a team, run things by Hunter before calling in favors."

"There's no pleasing you."

I rolled my eyes and stretched the phone cord far enough to reach Mr. Coffee. Only when my mug was full did I reply, "It's not about pleasing me. It's about keeping me out of prison."

"Don't be so dramatic. Hunter will take care of everything."

Hunter was an excellent lawyer, but he wasn't a wizard. He couldn't wave a magic wand and make a murder charge disappear. He couldn't explain how my gun ended up on the golf course. "We need to be circumspect in calling people like Uncle Jimmy."

She gave an aggrieved huff. "Fine. How was the party? I heard Harper the place looks like a hacienda."

"She did. The party was lovely."

You had more fun afterwards.

Geez. Make out in the kitchen for a few minutes and get endless guff. I gave Mr. Coffee the stink eye.

He chortled.

"What are you doing today?"

"I'm hoping to have coffee or lunch with Jessica Hendrick. There are also some last- minute errands I need to run before the kids go back to school."

"I want you and your family to come for dinner tonight."

"Mother—"

"Ellison, I insist." She'd cut me off before I could formulate an excuse. "This is not negotiable."

I knew when I was beat. "What time?"

"Five-thirty for drinks. We'll eat at six-fifteen."

There was no escaping this dinner. "Thank you for inviting us."

CHAPTER SEVEN

I settled onto the velvet sectional that dominated Jessica's living room, the plush cushions nearly swallowing me whole. The soft fabric was a rich shade of aubergine, and gold pillows abounded. The grasscloth-covered walls were also gold-hued. Together, the two colors were bold—they made a statement.

In the corner, a glass stereo cabinet hid a turntable. Apparently, Jessica was an Eagles fan. *Take It to the Limit* played softly.

Crossing my ankles, I folded my hands in my lap and let my gaze travel. A Frank Stella hung above the mantel. I'd once heard his work described as a jazz score on canvas. The interlocking geometric shapes were vibrant and crisp, improvised, yet precise. Like good jazz.

"Do you like it?" Jessica stood in the entrance to the living room, where she balanced a tray.

"I do."

"My husband loves it. We had the room designed around it."

As an artist, I could respect decorating around art. So often it worked the other way. People chose paintings that matched their couches or carpets. "It's striking."

Her mouth twitched, not a grimace (but close), and she sighed as if "striking" wasn't the adjective she wanted for her living room. "I have coffee."

"Bless you. And thank you for your invitation." When I'd called Jessica, she'd insisted on coffee at her home. Now that I was here, I was at a loss as to how to broach the subject of Prudence. My fingers itched to twist my rings. Instead, I smoothed my skirt and forced a smile.

Jessica settled the tray on the smoked-glass top of her brass coffee table. "Cream, right?"

"Just a jot."

She added a tiny spill of cream to the steaming cup and handed it to me.

"Thank you."

"You're welcome. Cookie?"

"I shouldn't."

"That just makes them taste better."

I selected a small cookie from the proffered plate and took a tiny bite.

Jessica put the plate down on the table and said, "I imagine you're here to talk about Prudence."

I choked on my cookie. Crumbs lodged themselves in my throat, and I clutched my neck as my eyes watered.

"Oh, my goodness! Are you okay?"

I nodded, not entirely sure. I could still breathe. That counted for something.

She offered me a napkin. "Would you like a glass of water?"

"Please," I gasped.

She hurried out of the room, and I used the napkin to dab at the skin beneath my eyes. Hopefully, my mascara wasn't too smudged. Looking like a raccoon didn't suit me.

Jessica returned with a glass of ice water.

I took it and sipped gratefully.

"You're sure you're okay?" she pressed.

The water had helped. "I'm fine."

"So, you are here about Prudence." She reclaimed her seat and leaned closer to me as if eavesdroppers lurked in the corners of her living room. "I heard you're a suspect in her murder."

The weight of the pending charge settled on my shoulders. Of course, she knew about the murder charge. Good news traveled fast. Bad news traveled faster. "Yes."

She sat back, shaking her head in disbelief. "There's not much I can tell you."

I hoped she was wrong. "You spent time together before you left for Michigan?"

Her lips pressed into a wire-thin line, and she tugged at one of her diamond earrings. "We did."

"Can you think of anyone who might have wanted her dead?"

Jessica stared into her coffee cup, her free fingers still turning the stud in her ear.

"Please?" I wasn't begging. Not really. I was totally begging.

Long seconds passed before she said, "We were at The Prospect having lunch when Nancy Fleetwood came to the table. She was furious with Prudence."

"Did she say why?"

"She blamed Prudence for her breakup with Hatton."

"What did Prudence say?"

"She was dismissive. We were seated, but she managed to look down her nose at Nancy, who was standing.

Jessica leaned forward, putting her coffee cup on the table, freeing her hands. Those she wrung. "After Nancy left, I asked what she'd done. Prudence shrugged and told me that Hatton had a right to know what kind of woman Nancy really was."

"Wow." What had Nancy done to end up in Prudence's crosshairs? Prudence was awful, but she usually directed that awfulness at me. Nancy was definitely on my list of possible killers.

Jessica nodded. "Exactly. It was mean. Petty. Even cruel. And frankly none of Prudence's business. Worse, she seemed genuinely pleased about Nancy's distress." Glancing down at her hands, her eyes widened as if she didn't realize what she'd been doing. "She seemed…smug."

I could picture the scene perfectly. The Prospect's wooden tables, the brick walls, the hanging ferns, the crusty bread baked and served in a miniature flowerpot, and Prudence's self-satisfied, horse-teethed smirk.

"After that lunch, I distanced myself. We even left early for Michigan."

"Is there anything else you can think of?"

Jessica looked at the ceiling, her coffee, the walls, the Stella, anywhere but me. "I hate to speak ill of the dead…"

"But?" I prompted when her silence lasted too long.

"It's probably nothing…"

I bit my tongue and waited.

"Lately, Prudence had more money. That day, she offered to pick up the check for lunch. In all the years I've known her, she'd never treated me to lunch. Either I paid, or we went Dutch. She had new clothes. Designer clothes. A diamond tennis bracelet. I wondered if there might be a new man in her life." She rolled her neck, carefully avoiding my avid gaze. "I wondered if he might be married."

"Does the name Fob mean anything to you?"

"No. Should it?"

"When Prudence and I argued at the club, she mentioned his name."

Jessica shook her head as a frown wrinkled her brow. "So, she was carrying on with a married man."

That shouldn't come as a surprise. Prudence made a habit of adultery. "You two were unlikely friends."

She chuckled softly. "We've known—knew—each other forever. Since Kitty's been gone, she's seemed so lonely. I hoped that maintaining at least one female friendship might mellow her."

"That was kind of you." And seriously misguided.

"It didn't work." Jessica's voice was filled with unexpected bitterness, and I couldn't help but wonder if Prudence had somehow wronged her as well.

WE SAT IN MOTHER AND DADDY'S DRIVEWAY, NONE OF US moving. The quiet car felt like a pressure cooker.

Grace, who'd had to cancel plans to accommodate her grandmother's dictate, stared straight ahead and radiated teenage frost —cold enough so that we didn't really need the air-conditioner. She wasn't speaking to me.

Beau, who'd spent the day at the pool, still smelled faintly of chlorine and suntan lotion. He was so tired his eyes were at half-mast.

Anarchy's brow was furrowed—there was something on his mind. Something serious. I could feel his tension like static in the air.

The front door opened, and Mother stepped onto the stoop.

No one in the car reached for a handle.

"We could run," Anarchy suggested. "This car is fast. We'd reach the state line before she has a chance to chase us."

"Very funny." I swallowed a sigh and girded my loins. "Let's do this."

"I prefer Anarchy's plan," said Grace.

My fingers closed around the metal handle. "We all like Anarchy's plan, but it's not feasible."

"You're no fun." At least she was speaking to me now.

"What's for dinner?" Beau's voice was wary, edged with the

trauma of his last culinary experience at Mother and Daddy's. She'd served liver and onions and sauteed spinach. Not exactly kid favorites.

"I'm sure it'll be delicious," I lied as I opened my door and swung my feet onto the drive, the warmth of the concrete seeping through the soles of my sandals.

Anarchy followed suit. "I'll take you to Topsy's after dinner." Topsy's was Beau's favorite ice cream shop. The Brookside store also sold a mean popcorn ball.

Placated, Beau opened his door.

Grace was immune to sugar-based bribery. She remained in the backseat.

"Please, honey. We won't stay late. And if you want to go out afterwards, I'll extend your curfew by thirty minutes."

"For good?"

"One night only."

She huffed, but she opened her door.

The four of us dragged our feet to the front stoop. I'd seen happier faces on pallbearers.

Mother tapped her foot and sent me a death glare. "You're late."

"It's five-thirty-two."

"Late."

"My apologies, Mother. I have a few things going on."

Ignoring my sarcasm, she turned on her heel and disappeared into the house, expecting us to follow.

"She's really mad at you," Grace whispered.

"She's worried. She gets prickly when she's worried."

"I'm glad you don't do that."

My heart warmed. "Thanks, sweetheart."

We turned right into the living room, where the lush oriental rug muted the sound of our steps. Stargazer lilies in a crystal vase perfume the air. I'd been in plenty of lovely homes, but— hands down—Mother's was the most elegant.

Which made sense. Mother, with her Chanel No. 5 and St. John suits, was ridiculously elegant.

In the corner, Daddy stood next to the polished walnut bar cart. Crystal decanters were lined up like soldiers, each with a gleaming sterling charm around its neck declaring the contents—bourbon, scotch, gin, vodka.

"Anarchy, what'll it be? Beer?"

"Bourbon. Neat."

Daddy's eyebrows rose. Mine too. Anarchy rarely drank hard liquor.

"What about you, Ellison?"

"Chardonnay, please."

"Grace? Beau?"

The kids requested soft drinks, and we all found our places.

Beau, who'd picked a seat near the coffee table, eyed the ramekin of spreadable Braunschweiger like it might attack him. The pinkish-brown meat wasn't Mother's usual fare. To plebeian. To ethnic.

"A German appetizer before a German meal," said Mother, martini glass in hand. "We're having veal schnitzel and creamed cabbage for dinner."

Beau shot me a look of quiet desperation.

Poor kid. You'd think Mother would serve steaks or fried chicken when we came for dinner.

"Really? Maybe we should call for pizza."

"Ellison Russell—"

"Jones." Correcting her had become automatic. "Why German food, Mother?"

"We're broadening our horizons." Her tone clearly conveyed her displeasure. With me. How dare I suggest pizza when her cook had gone to all this trouble?

Anarchy caught Beau's worried gaze and mouthed, "Topsy's."

Mother's lips narrowed. She'd seen his silent promise, but

rather than call him out, she asked, "Did you speak with Jessica Hendrick?"

"I did."

"What did she say?" Now, her tone was laced with impatience.

I did not want to discuss the case in front of the children, but I had to tell her something. Otherwise, she'd poke at me all night. "Prudence made an enemy of Nancy Fleetwood."

Mother nodded. Prudence's making enemies came as no surprise. "How?"

I glanced at the children and shook my head.

She pursed her lips, annoyed with my reticence. "Have you told Hunter?"

I accepted a glass of wine from Daddy and took a quick, grateful sip. "Not yet."

Mother cut her gaze toward Anarchy. "Ellison, you must tell him. Call him as soon as you get home. Hunter has your best interests at heart." Her inference was clear.

Anarchy crossed to the bar cart, accepted a glass of bourbon from my father's hands, and gave Mother a look I hoped he never directed at me. "Are you suggesting I don't?"

Mother blinked. Twice. She hadn't expected him to stand up to her. "Of course not."

"Frannie knows we're all in Ellison's corner. Don't you, dear?" Daddy's voice carried a not-so-subtle warning.

"That's right." She offered a tight smile. "What did you do today, Anarchy?"

"I talked to Courtland Gerhardt. Thought he might know if anyone at the club had it in for Prudence."

"And?"

"He gave me a list."

"Well," Mother prompted, "who's on it?"

"It's a long list."

"Does Detective Morrison have that list?" She wrinkled her

nose as if she'd just smelled something off in the kitchen. In a word, dinner. "I must say, your colleague's rush to charge Ellison with a crime has been most distressing."

"I agree entirely," Anarchy said evenly.

"I'll be taking it up with the department once Ellison is cleared."

"Mother!" Having Mother target someone in the homicide division wouldn't make Anarchy popular with the other detectives.

"What, Ellison? The man obviously carries some sort of grudge, and it's clouding what little judgment he has."

I glanced at the kids. Grace had sunk deep into a brocade club chair. Beau seemed hypnotized by the Braunschweiger. But they were both listening. It was time to change the subject. "How was your day, Daddy? Did you play golf?"

"Birdied three, six, eleven. Bogeyed five, twelve, fourteen, and seventeen. Parred the rest."

"Well done."

He grinned and swirled his scotch around the single over-sized ice cube in his glass. "We need to get you back out on the course."

"When things calm down," I promised.

"You too, Anarchy." Daddy gave Anarchy's shoulder a pat. "Have you been practicing?"

"Whenever I have free time." Which was never.

"We'll make a golfer of you yet."

Mother, who considered golf a good walk spoiled, huffed. "What are you going to do about Nancy Fleetwood?"

"I suppose I'll talk to her."

Anarchy frowned at me. "We'll give her name to the police."

"Along with everyone else on the long list?" Mother's lips curled into a dismissive sneer. "When will they get around to talking to her?"

Anarchy's eyes narrowed. He leaned forward, picked up the

tiny silver knife next to the Braunschweiger and aggressively spread the smoked liverwurst across a piece of melba toast.

Mother had gotten to him.

"Do you really think that dreadful man is going to put any effort into identifying other suspects?" she demanded.

Anarchy bit into the canapé.

"He won't. I know his type. There's a two-by-four on his shoulder, and he wants to make an example of Ellison." Mother's gaze traveled the room. "Grace, sit up."

Grace, who was unhappily merging with the club chair, shot me a murderous look before she straightened her spine.

"If you and Ellison want the killer caught, you'll have to do it yourselves. It's the only option. One of you needs to talk to Nancy Fleetwood. And everyone else on Courtland's list." Mother's eyes narrowed, daring Anarchy to argue. "Since you've been warned off the investigation, that leaves my daughter."

Annoyingly, Mother wasn't wrong.

CHAPTER EIGHT

We stopped in Brookside on our way home, parking near the top of the hill so that we had to walk past The Studio (my favorite needlepoint shop) and The Dime Store before we reached Topsy's. A line stretched out the door.

No one, not even Grace, who was eager to meet her friends, suggested skipping it. We were all hungry. Mother's foray into German cuisine had been less than satisfying, and we'd spent more time pushing food around our plates than eating.

"What are you in the mood for?" Anarchy ruffled Beau's hair.

"Rocky road."

"What about you, Grace?"

"Strawberry."

"Ellison?"

"Mint chocolate chip."

His eyebrows lifted. My usual order was a diet limeade.

"Let's pray Mother never serves veal schnitzel again."

"Amen," Grace muttered.

"Ellison, is that you?"

I turned, a polite smile already on my face, and found Cricket Hubbell and her husband standing behind me.

Hubb leaned in to kiss my cheek, and I blinked at the sudden onslaught of Paco Rabanne Pour Homme, wrinkling my nose at the herbal, woodsy scent. The cologne wasn't bad (in fact, I rather liked it), but there was a lot of it. I couldn't help but wonder if Hubb was the man I'd overheard at Harper's party. Was he on Courtland's list of club members who'd held grudges against Prudence?

That was ridiculous. If I suspected every man who wore Paco Rabanne, my list of potential killers would be longer than my arm. "Hubb, have you met my husband? Anarchy, this is John Hubbell."

Hubb held out his hand. "Hubb to my friends."

The two men shook, sizing each other up.

"There must be a story that goes with your name. I'd love to hear it." Hubb was a charmer. Tall and rangy, Hubb looked elegant in anything he wore and made friends everywhere he went.

Cricket pulled me in for a hug and whispered, "I'm so glad to see you out. I know, I know there was bad blood between you and Prudence, but no one believes you'd kill her."

Except for Detective Morrison and the prosecutor. I forced a smile.

The line inched forward. Not fast enough.

It hurt to keep the smile fixed on my face. "Thank you for saying so."

"You're all dressed up." Cricket waved her hand at my linen shift, Anarchy and Beau's navy blazers, and Grace's Lilly dress.

"We had dinner with Mother and Daddy."

By contrast, Cricket and Hubb looked cool and comfortable. She wore a gauzy red cotton sundress. Her husband wore faded Madras shorts, a pink polo shirt, and loafers without socks.

"How's Frances holding up?" she asked.

"Nothing fazes Mother." Except having her daughter charged with murder.

"She's a force, that's for sure."

We stepped forward. It was our turn, but the teenage boy behind the counter stared at Grace with a glazed look in his eyes. Anarchy had to repeat our order three times.

Grace didn't seem to notice the boy's attention.

Cricket chuckled softly. "She's a pretty girl."

"And a smart one."

"Pretty will take her farther." Cricket had been a pretty girl, and she'd landed a lawyer. She remained a pretty woman, but I got the impression that she and Hubb were amiable roommates, not actual partners. To be fair, that kind of relationship wasn't unusual. Half the married women in my circle stayed with men who were as comfortable (and exciting) as broken-in slippers. Their marriages puttered along, and no one complained. Well, not too much. Why risk financial straits when things weren't terrible?

Thanks to an inheritance from her father and my success, Grace would never have to depend on a man to take care of her financially. She could pursue a career that excited her. She could stay single (although I hoped she found love). She could make a mark. "Pretty can fade. Smart is forever."

Cricket's smile turned brittle.

Had I offended her? If so, it was unintentional. After all, Cricket's pretty hadn't faded. Yet.

Anarchy handed Beau his cone. Grace's strawberry cone came next. Then mine.

I licked the edge where the ice cream had already started to melt. The sudden sweetness tingled across my tongue. "Cricket, it was lovely to see you." There were people lined up outside, and we needed to make room for them.

"Let's get together soon. Are you and Anarchy free for dinner next week?"

I was a murder suspect, and she was asking us to dinner? Cricket and I weren't close, but a sudden wave of affection had me nodding. "I'd like that. May I call you after I check my calendar?"

"Of course." She kissed the air next to my cheek. "We'll talk tomorrow."

~

I SAT AT THE KITCHEN ISLAND, MY PEN TAPPING A STEADY rhythm against the pad of paper in front of me.

Problem? Thanks to Mr. Coffee, the delicious aroma of fresh-brewed coffee hung heavy in the air.

"I'm not sure what's most important."

Write everything down, then rank the order of importance. Mr. Coffee gave the best advice.

I took a sip of coffee, savoring the slightly bitter taste, and wrote, *Call Nancy Fleetwood.* I felt Mr. Coffee's curiosity, but he remained quiet—he was too polite to pry. *Call Hunter.* I tapped my pen against the monogrammed pad and added, *Call Cricket.* Then there were the errands—when Beau and I went back-to-school shopping, we'd forgotten to buy wide magic markers. That required a stop at The Dime Store. Grace was out of conditioner (which was somehow my fault). The drugstore in Prairie Village was the only place that carried her hard-to-find favorite brand.

Dime Store. Bruce Smith's.

The scratch of my pen disturbed Max. He lifted his head from his paws and stared at me as if I'd wronged him. I hadn't. He and Finn had already had a nice walk, twice around Loose Park. And treats. More treats than were strictly healthy.

How was dinner last night?

I answered with a dry laugh.

That bad?

"Mother served veal schnitzel." I took another sip of coffee. "When Grace realized she was eating a baby cow, she cried. Even worse, Mother picked a fight with Anarchy."

She's worried. Mr. Coffee had a point. A small one.

"That doesn't explain the schnitzel."

Mr. Coffee gave a sympathetic gurgle. *When does Aggie get back?*

"This afternoon." Even though I knew there were hours and hours until her arrival, I glanced at the clock. Life was easier with Aggie around.

Did you decide what's first?

I blinked and returned my focus to the list in front of me. "Nancy. I'll call Hunter after I talk to her." Better to ask forgiveness than permission.

I stood, my bare feet whispering against the cool floor.

Where are you going?

"I need to look up Nancy's number. She works." Not that I had her home number handy. I offered Mr. Coffee a grateful smile, topped off my mug, inhaled the little puff of steam, and then headed for the family room, my desk, and the yellow pages. The pages were thin, almost flimsy, and the writing seemed smaller than usual. It took me several minutes to locate the number. When I had it, I dialed.

"Brewster Manufacturing, how may I help you?" The woman's voice was warm, almost happy, as if she was thrilled to help sell flanges.

"May I please speak with Nancy Fleetwood?"

"May I tell her who's calling?"

"Ellison Jones."

"Hold, please."

I drummed my nails on my desk while I waited. Anarchy might not be happy about this call, but Mother was right— Detective Morrison was convinced of my guilt. He wasn't investigating anyone else. If I wanted answers, I had to get them myself.

"Ellison?"

"Nancy." Anything I'd planned on saying evaporated. "Good morning."

"Good morning. How may I help you?"

"May I take you to lunch?"

"Is this about Prudence?"

"Yes."

She sighed. "I can't today. My car is in the shop—"

"I'll pick you up." I sounded too eager, almost desperate.

She was silent for so long I was sure she was going to turn me down. "Fine."

I suppressed a relieved sigh. "Perfect. What time?"

"Noon. I'll meet you at the front entrance."

"Thank you for this."

"Don't mention it. That woman ruins lives from beyond the grave." She wasn't wrong.

"See you at noon."

We hung up, and I reached for my address book, quickly flipping to the page with Cricket's number.

On the third ring, someone answered. "Hubbell residence."

"May I please speak with Mrs. Hubbell?"

"This is she." Cricket's words were clipped, her voice cool.

"Cricket, it's Ellison."

"Ellison!" Warmth flooded down the line. "I'm so glad you called. Have you checked your calendar?"

"The kids go back to school next week. I think we should be around for dinner those first few nights. Next weekend?"

"Are you free tonight?"

It was on the tip of my tongue to say "no," but Cricket had been so kind, and there was no reason not to go. "We are." Aggie would feed the kids—pizza or lasagna or tacos. Beau would vote for pizza.

"Perfect. Six-thirty at the club?"

"The club?" I already felt the stares boring into my skin.

"Why not? Everyone knows you're innocent."

"I appreciate your faith." But I didn't share it. I bet loads of people were whispering about my guilt.

"Trust me, as many people who hated Prudence, her killer might get a medal."

That wasn't belief in my innocence. That was schadenfreude —taking pleasure in Prudence's misfortune. "I didn't kill her."

"Which is why we should dine at the club, to prove to everyone that you don't care about the rumors. Because. You're. Innocent."

Did Cricket and Hubb need to meet their food minimum for the quarter? I quickly dismissed the thought. Cricket meant well. She was trying to be helpful. "Fine. We'll see you at six-thirty."

Three hours later, I pulled into the Brewster Manufacturing's lot, parked in a spot reserved for visitors, and waited. When the clock on the dash read five minutes after the hour, I got out of my car and went inside.

A receptionist looked at me as if my arrival was a surprise.

"I'm here to see Nancy Fleetwood."

She nodded as if I'd cleared up a mystery. "One moment, I'll call her office."

"Ellison, is that you?" Fred Brewster had entered the lobby, and he stared at me as if he couldn't imagine what had brought me there.

"Fred! How nice to see you."

"Likewise." He leaned in to kiss me on the cheek, and a wave of Paco Rabanne Pour Homme assaulted my nose. Was everyone wearing it now? And in volume?

"Pam is quite the hero."

His sharp brown eyes widened, and he tilted his head. "Oh?"

"She didn't tell you? She dove into the pool and saved a little girl."

"She didn't mention it. But she's been so upset by the murder on the golf course, it probably slipped her mind." He smoothed the lapels of his plaid sports coat. "Awful business."

"Agreed."

"What brings you here?"

"I'm having lunch with—"

"Sorry to keep you waiting!" Nancy swept into the lobby, spotted me with Fred, and slowed her steps. "You two know each other?"

"Pam used to babysit my daughter," I explained. "Grace's favorite sitter of all time."

"Well, the admiration was mutual. If all kids were like Grace, Pam might have continued babysitting."

Grace had been as easy kid. Happy to eat frozen pizza for dinner, play a board game, watch TV, and go to bed.

"You're having lunch?" he asked.

I nodded.

"Well, have a nice time. Nancy, I'll see you later this afternoon."

She gave Fred a wooden nod before grabbing my elbow and leading me out of the building.

"Where to?" I figured she knew the neighborhood better than I did.

"Honestly, any place that serves a decent glass of wine. I'm having a day."

"Poor Freddie's in the River Quay?"

"Perfect."

We drove the short distance without saying much, choosing to listen to Glen Campbell sing about the dirty sidewalks of Broadway.

I parked near the restaurant, and we walked to the entrance in silence. A silence that was becoming awkward.

A hostess led us to a table near the window overlooking Delaware Street, and we perused our menus as if our lives depended on it. Poor Freddie's, which took up the ground floor of a historic building, served sandwiches and pastas and pizza. My choice was easy. I put my menu on the table and cleared my throat, ready to launch into an awkward conversation.

"What may I get you to drink?" The waitress, who gave us a sunny smile, had offered me a brief reprieve.

"Chardonnay," Nancy replied.

"Two, please." I didn't usually drink at lunch, but a glass of wine sounded too good to pass up.

When the waitress left us, Nancy eyed me carefully. "You're having a day, too?"

I stared at the woman across the table. Her dark blonde hair was pulled back in a low ponytail, and her face looked taut. "I'm having a week."

She laughed softly. "I suppose you are."

"You heard."

That earned a wry grin. "I don't live under a rock."

"I don't either."

Her face shuttered. "You heard about Hatton."

"I heard."

"I hated Prudence, but I didn't kill her."

I didn't think she had. Mainly because I couldn't imagine how she might have taken my gun. We were barely acquaintances. She'd never been in my house. And we ran with different sets—there was no one to tell her I kept my .22 in my nightstand. "I believe you."

She blinked. "So why are we here?"

"What did Prudence do to you?"

Her gaze fell to the table's glossy surface. "Let's wait for the wine."

The waitress appeared a moment later, dropped off two Chardonnays, and took our lunch orders. A Reuben for me, a Tom Sawyer pizza for Nancy.

Nancy took a sip, exhaled slowly, deliberately, and then took another sip. Her gaze fixed on the sidewalk where a young mother pushed a stroller. "She tried to blackmail me."

I gaped across the table. "Pardon?"

"You heard me." She still avoided my gaze. "Prudence knew that when I was single, before I started dating Hatton, I visited a club in the West Bottoms."

"Club K?"

She snapped her attention away from the window, surprise flashing in her pale blue eyes. "You've been?"

"Not exactly." I owned the building that housed it. "I've met Mistress K."

"Henry."

"Henry." On my lips, my late husband's name was a curse word.

"Prudence demanded two-thousand dollars, or she'd tell Hatton."

"You chose not to pay."

"Telling him I'd been there was as good as admitting she'd been there, too. And even if she did tell him, my sexual history is my own. Hatton knew there had been other men after my ex. We talked about it." A bitter chuckle ruffled the surface of the wine she held near her lips. "It wasn't as if he lived like a monk."

"He wasn't expecting…kink."

"He was not. It didn't matter that I hadn't been to the club recently. That I ever went was too much for him." She put her glass down hard enough for wine to slosh over the rim. "I cared about him. I was counting on a future together. And Prudence ruined that."

"You couldn't explain—"

"He didn't want to hear it."

"I'm sorry."

"Yeah, me too."

The waitress arrived with our food, asking, "Another glass?"

"I've got to go back to work." Regret colored her reply.

"I'm driving."

The sunny waitress nodded and left us to our lunches.

I picked up my sandwich and took a bite, barely suppressing a moan. "This is marvelous."

Nancy, who was chewing a bite of pizza, nodded her agreement before asking, "Who do you think killed her?"

"Well, if she tried to blackmail you, odds are good she tried to blackmail others." Odds were better than good. Jessica had mentioned that Prudence had been flush with cash.

"And someone killed her for it." Nancy put down her pizza and took a healthy swig of wine.

All I had to do was figure out if any of Prudence's targets might have known where I kept my gun.

"I have to ask." Nancy rested her folded hands on the table's edge. "Did Jessica tell you about me?"

I didn't reply. But my silence spoke volumes.

"Because if you're looking for someone who hated Prudence…"

"Really?"

Nancy nodded, reclaiming her slice. "Prudence had set her sights on Jessica's husband. That's why Jessica insisted they leave for Michigan a month early."

"I had no idea."

She nodded with more vigor. "Jessica thought it prudent to avoid a potential problem."

"Prudence moved on." But had Jessica known that? Had she still worried that Prudence wanted her husband? "Prudence was seeing someone named Fob."

"What kind of name is that?"

In all honesty, I had plenty of friends with odd nicknames. I was married to a man named Anarchy. Fob wasn't that crazy. "An odd one. I'm hoping someone recognizes it."

She shook her head. "Sorry. You'll have to keep looking."

"Do you think Prudence might have blackmailed other people who visited Club K?"

"You know Henry went there?"

"Oh, I'm well aware." Impossible to keep the bitterness out of my voice.

"The only people I ever recognized there were with him—Prudence, Kitty, Madeline."

"So, if she was blackmailing someone in our set, it wasn't over Club K."

"Unless Prudence recognized someone I didn't." Her cheeks flushed. "But even then, it would only have been Prudence's word."

"She didn't have proof?"

"It's not as if Mistress K allows cameras."

"Then Hatton…"

"He asked me, and I told the truth. I refused to lie to him."

"He missed out on an amazing woman." Nancy was pretty and smart and financially independent and honest. Hatton English was a fool to have let her go.

"That's nice of you to say."

"Nothing less than the truth."

We moved on to other topics, and by the time we finished lunch I felt as if I'd made a friend.

When I dropped Nancy at her office, she paused before getting out of the car. "I'm glad you called, Ellison. If I think of anything that might help, I'll call you."

I sat in the car after she disappeared inside the building, my fingers flexing and releasing the steering wheel. Club K was only a few minutes away, and it was time to visit my least favorite tenant.

CHAPTER NINE

I parked in front of the single building in my real estate empire (an old warehouse in the West Bottoms) and gathered the courage to knock on its door. I would rather pick a fight with Mother, waste a whole afternoon debating vegetables on the kids' buffet with Anne Everist, or spend a night in a jail cell than knock on that door. With the clang of the cell door closing still reverberating through my memory, that was saying something.

Given that I didn't want to spend multiple nights in a jail cell, I forced myself out of the car.

The drone of cicadas meant the sound of my knuckles meeting the door's thick surface was barely audible. My stomach churned, and I regretted eating the entire Reuben at Poor Freddie's. The temptation to return to my car and drive away was real. Instead, I waited a full minute before knocking again—louder this time.

The door swung open, and Club K's proprietress gazed at me with an amused smirk on her shiny red lips. "Seersucker."

"Is that any way to greet your landlord, Kathleen?"

She winced at the use of her actual name. "What do you want?"

"Prudence Davies."

She rolled her eyes and opened the door wide enough to let me in.

I did my best to avoid looking at the apparatuses in the space. I couldn't imagine what most of them were for. I didn't want to. Not that I wanted to look at Kathleen either. She wore a high, sleek ponytail, dramatic make-up, a black leather bustier, and she'd tucked the tightest black pants I'd ever seen into knee-high high-heeled boots.

"Still blushing."

"You say that like blushing is a bad thing."

"It is around here." She glanced at her watch—a gold Rolex encrusted with diamonds. "I have a client on his way. What has Prudence done now?"

"She was murdered."

Kathleen's dark brows winged toward her hairline. "Well, that's a surprise."

"She was blackmailing people she saw here." No one wanted their sexual kinks whispered about at cocktail parties. They'd pay to keep spanking or whips or crawling private.

"Who?"

"Nancy Fleetwood, for one."

"Strong woman." Kathleen nodded as if she approved. "She was well on her way to being a great dominatrix when she decided the lifestyle wasn't for her."

Unbidden, unwanted, the vision of Nancy in black leather with a whip in her hand invaded my brain. I couldn't unimagine that. "Wow."

"You're blushing again."

Of course, I was blushing. Blushing was a perfectly normal response to learning the woman with whom one had just lunched with wielded a mean riding crop. Blushing or horror. Maybe both. "Who else might Prudence have blackmailed?"

Kathleen shook her head. She didn't know, or she refused to tell me?

"I'm not looking for your entire client list."

"Then who are you looking for?"

"The clients I might know." The clients who might know enough about me to sneak into my house and steal my gun.

"And why would I give you that information?"

"Because I was arrested for Prudence's murder." My voice was flat.

Her eyes widened. "Still not seeing a reason to tell you."

"If I go to jail, my husband will be managing this building." The last thing she'd want was a cop associated with her club. "And he'll be relentless in trying to prove my innocence. He might even subpoena your entire client list."

She pursed her glossy lips. "Trip Selden."

Trip and his wife Lucia were definitely amiable roommates. Frankly, it wasn't a stretch to imagine him straying. But kink? "Really?"

"No, I made it up," she deadpanned.

"I just—"

"Why does it continue to surprise you when people want more than vanilla sex?"

Because I tried not to think about other people's sex lives. But now, thanks to Prudence, I had to. "Just Trip?"

"He's the only one I can think of." She glanced again at her watch. "Unless you want to help me welcome my next client—" she paused, taking in the fresh color on my cheeks with amuse-ment dancing in her eyes "—you should go."

"Fine." I strode to the door.

"Ellison."

Her voice stopped me. The air, already thick with the scents of leather and scotch and spent desire, felt heavy. Portentous.

"Anyone who thinks you're capable of murder is an idiot. If I think of anything else, I'll contact you."

I didn't believe her. "I appreciate that." Without a backward glance, I stepped outside, hurrying to my car and sliding behind the wheel.

Trip Selden?

I slid the key into the ignition and started the engine, grateful for the sudden blast of cold air.

Lucia Selden had been inside my house plenty of times, and her daughter and Grace were friends. It was possible that Courtney had told her mother about my gun. Had Lucia told Trip? Or had Lucia taken the weapon? Would she kill Prudence to avoid the embarrassment of her husband's proclivities being revealed?

I rested my forehead against the steering wheel, not lifting it until the slam of a car door interrupted my circling thoughts. Glancing out the window, my jaw dropped. Kathleen had lied. Trip wasn't the only member of our set with a Club K problem.

I'd take that up with her later. For now, I put the car in gear and drove away.

~

"YOU'RE HOME." AGGIE MET ME AT THE DOOR, A SWIRL OF mustard-colored muumuu and sproingy red hair. Her welcoming smile reached from ear to ear.

I launched myself at her, hugging her tightly. "I am so glad you're home." Her absence had been felt, and her return was a comfort I didn't realize I'd been craving.

She patted my back gently. "Things here have been…challenging?"

"You heard?"

"Mrs. Walford has called three times. She mentioned a murder charge."

I bet she had. "Then you realize 'challenging' is an under-statement." We separated. "How was your trip?"

"Wonderful. Relaxing. Perfect." Aggie's expression turned dreamy.

I took a surreptitious glance at her left hand and found her ring finger bare. An incredibly selfish pang of relief shot through me. I wanted Aggie to be happy (she certainly deserved it), but the thought of her marrying her beau and leaving us…well, I didn't know how we'd function without her. She was more than a housekeeper. She was part of our family. "I'm glad you enjoyed yourself. Did anyone else call?"

"Hunter Tafft wants to speak with you at your earliest convenience. Also, a woman named Darla Higgins would like to speak with you."

"My cellmate."

"Look at you making jailhouse cronies." Aggie's amusement was obvious.

"Just the one. You'd like her."

She tilted her head. "What was she in for?"

"Smashing up her boss's car with a Louisville Slugger."

Her eyebrows lifted. "He deserved it?"

"He did. I asked Hunter to help her."

"She's probably calling to thank you."

I shrugged. "Maybe. I offered her a job."

Her eyebrows lifted even higher.

"Don't worry. I won't be forcing her into an affair and then firing her when my wife finds out. My car is safe."

Aggie's eyebrows drew together, and her lips thinned. "Poor girl."

I didn't have the energy to worry about Darla right now. "Hunter or Mother?"

"Hunter," she replied without hesitation. "Your mother can't keep you out of prison. Do you want coffee?"

"Iced tea, please." Much as I loved coffee, my cheeks were

still flushed from my trip to Club K, and I wanted something cool. I headed toward my desk in the family room and dialed Hunter's number with trembling fingers.

"Tafft."

"It's me. Ellison."

"Good. We've got lots to talk about."

A shiver of dread worked its way from the top of my head to the tip of my toes. "Okay." I drew the word out as if it could protect me from bad news.

"Your case goes to the grand jury next week."

My heart stuttered. "What does that mean?"

"Steele will present the case against you to the grand jury. If they come back with a true bill, you'll be charged with murder."

I should have asked Aggie for something stronger than iced tea. My throat felt tight, and my jaw ached with the sudden need to cry. Charged with murder. Me. Hearing Hunter talk about next steps made my position all too real. I swallowed around a lump. "What's a true bill?"

"It's a bill of indictment found by a grand jury. It means they believe there's sufficient evidence to justify a hearing of the case."

"Oh." There wasn't enough air in my lungs to say anything more.

Aggie appeared in the doorway holding a tall glass garnished with mint and lemon. "Are you okay? You're the color of old bones."

My eyes filled with stinging tears, and I shook my head.

She hurried to my side, depositing the tea on my desk, and taking my free hand in hers. The squeeze of her fingers gave me courage, and I asked, my voice hardly a whisper, "What do we do?"

"There's nothing we can do about the grand jury, but we'll keep looking for exonerating evidence and other suspects. You're innocent, Ellison."

"Are you telling me innocent people don't get convicted?" The question was too sharp. Hunter didn't deserve my newfound cynicism.

"Not with me as their lawyer."

I appreciated his confidence. I even managed a small watery smile. "I had lunch with Nancy Fleetwood today. Prudence tried to blackmail her. When Nancy refused to pay, Prudence wrecked Nancy's relationship with Hatton English."

Aggie gave another comforting squeeze before releasing my hand. Then she retreated a few steps, perching on the back of the couch. A silent (entirely welcome) observer.

"So, she had a motive."

"How often do people kill for revenge?"

"I don't have the answer to that."

"I don't think Nancy did it. Before she left for Michigan, Jessica Hendrick noticed that Prudence was flush with cash. I bet she was blackmailing someone else."

"Who?"

"Trip Selden."

Hunter knew Trip, and I could practically hear the cogs in my lawyer's brain turning. "Why do you say that?"

"He goes to Club K. Prudence saw him there."

"How do you know?"

"I stopped by earlier today and talked to the owner."

"Ellison!" He sounded genuinely alarmed.

"What?"

"You shouldn't have gone to a place like that."

I rolled my eyes. If only he knew how many times I'd had to visit Club K, he wouldn't sound so shocked. "Also, I overheard a conversation when I was at Harper's party." I quickly recounted what I'd heard in the alcove.

"You have no idea who was speaking?"

"Nope. Just lots of Paco Rabanne."

"Does Trip Selden wear that?"

"I've never noticed." But the next time I was near him, I'd be sniffing like a bloodhound.

"About Jessica Hendrick…"

"What about her?"

"She insisted on leaving early for Michigan because Prudence was making moves on her husband."

"You said Prudence was having an affair with someone named Fob."

"I'm not sure Jessica knew that."

He grunted softly. "Having other suspects—other motives—is great, but we still need to explain how the killer got your gun."

"Lucia and Trip Selden's daughter is friends with Grace. It's possible Grace told Courtney about my gun." I'd have to ask Grace when I saw her.

"And Courtney told her parents? When would they have had access to your house?"

"When Aggie was gone, we weren't the best about locking up. We're all so used to having her home that we often neglected to lock the doors."

"The dogs?"

"Easily bribed." A few cubes of steak, a few bites of hamburger, a biscuit or two—they weren't picky. "If Max had already met the thief—the killer—who stole my gun, they might not need a bribe." Max recognized friends.

"There's another angle we need to consider." Hunter's voice had dropped. Somehow—impossibly—he sounded even more serious.

I blinked back fresh, worried tears. "What's that?"

"It's possible someone is trying to frame you for Prudence's murder."

"What do you mean?" I wiped my eyes with the back of my hand, deliberately refusing to catch the gist dangling right in front of me.

"Someone killed her to get to you." His words came as a physical blow.

"You mean the killer didn't care about her death? They just want me to take the fall?" A pit opened in my stomach, and I pressed my free palm against my chest. Hunter's suggestion was every bit as bad as being accused of murder. Worse. If he was right, guilt would eat at me for the rest of my life. Guilt over Prudence. A totally inappropriate giggle threatened to escape my chest. I ruthlessly tamped it down.

"It's a possibility."

"Who hates me that much?"

"You've helped put a lot of people behind bars over the past year. It's possible one of their family members holds a grudge."

Oh, dear Lord. I lowered my head to my desk blotter as an unwelcome parade of killers flashed against the backs of my eyelids.

"Ellison?"

"Give me a minute. Please."

"Of course."

"Have you mentioned this theory to Anarchy?" I asked.

"He's reviewing the cases now."

They'd talked about my case without me. I glanced at Aggie and mouthed, "Wine, please."

She nodded and disappeared into the kitchen.

I sat up, leaned my head back until I was staring at the ceiling, and gathered my tattered courage. "To recap, Prudence was a blackmailer. That might have gotten her killed. She was having an affair with a married man. That also might have gotten her killed. Or someone murdered her to frame me. Those theories leave us with too many suspects to count. And none of those suspects matter, because the prosecutor will be taking the case to the grand jury next week. When they hear about the argument at the pool, my lack of an alibi, and that my gun was used to kill her, I'll be charged with murder."

"Unless we identify the killer before the grand jury convenes, yes."

"Then that's what we'll do." Confidence laced my voice. It was a sham. Inside I was a quivering mess. I straightened my shoulders, ignored my jellied innards, and forced a smile that Hunter couldn't see. "We'll find the killer."

CHAPTER TEN

"Ellison?" Libba's voice carried from the kitchen.

"Family room." My voice sounded thin and reedy. "Is there anything else?" I asked Hunter. My knuckles ached from holding the receiver too tightly.

"No. I'll be in touch. Keep your chin up."

Right. I managed a humorless smile and hung up the phone as Libba appeared holding two glasses of wine. Her sharp gaze took me in—the undoubtedly red-rimmed eyes, the tight set of my jaw, the tremor in my hands—and her expression softened. "How are you holding up?"

My traitorous eyes filled, blurring her face. I couldn't seem to speak, so I shook my head.

"That bad?" she asked gently, stepping closer.

I was days away from being charged with murder in open court. The reality pressed against my chest until I felt flattened. "That bad," I whispered, the words catching in my throat.

"Here." She pushed a wine glass into my hand. "You need this."

I shouldn't be drinking, not after the wine at lunch, not with all I needed to do. But I took a shaky sip, silently vowing to keep my wits about me tomorrow. This afternoon, I wanted to lean on my best friend and pretend my biggest problem was the lack of vegetables on the kids' buffet at the end-of-summer party on Sunday night. "How are you?"

"Same old, same old. Charlie wants to get married."

"I still don't see the problem."

Unexpected vulnerability flashed in her eyes. "I never pictured myself married."

"Is that your only objection?"

"There are details I need to share with Charlie. When he hears them, he may change his mind."

"I seriously doubt that. The man is crazy about you."

A sweet smile curled her lips. "He is something special."

"If he makes you happy, hold on to him."

She shook her head, "I'm not here to talk about me. How can I help you?"

"Have you given Fob any thought?" Finding Prudence's mystery man might help my case.

"I've racked my brain, and I've never heard that name before. It must be Prudence's pet name for whatever sad sack fell for her. I'm sorry."

I deflated. At this rate, we'd never find him. "Have you heard anything funny about Lucia or Trip Selden?" I asked, pushing forward.

"Funny?" Libba was better friends with Lucia than I was. "They got back from Greece last week. They took all five children. They island hopped, sailed around the Aegean, visited ruins, and ate so much moussaka that Lucia worried they'd turn into eggplants. She said they had a fabulous time."

"They were in town when Prudence was killed?" I pressed.

Her brow furrowed. "Why do you ask?"

"How well do you know Nancy Fleetwood?"

"Not well. She's always seemed nice enough." She

scrunched up her face. "Ugly divorce. I think she came out well. What does Nancy Fleetwood have to do with the Seldens?"

"We had lunch today. Prudence tried to blackmail her, and Nancy told her to go to hell."

"Good woman." She frowned. "What did Nancy do to attract Horse-teeth's attention?"

I shook my head. "It's none of our business."

Libba stuck out her tongue. "You're no fun."

"The point is Prudence was blackmailing people—or at least trying to."

"Trip Selden?"

"Possibly. Any rumors of trouble in paradise?" Jinx would know for sure, but she'd ask what Prudence had held over Trip's head.

"So, you didn't mean funny, you meant salacious. The answer is no. Honestly, who else would want him?" Libba wrinkled her nose. "The mid-life crisis on that man."

"What do you mean?"

"He started working out at a gym, colored his hair, and bought new clothes. None of it makes a difference. Worse, he marinates in Paco Rabanne. I swear my eyes water whenever I'm around him. I don't know how Lucia stands it."

More Paco Rabanne. Trip Selden was looking more and more like a suspect.

"Mom?" Grace hollered.

"Family room," I called.

She appeared wearing shorts and a T-shirt, red-faced, and dripping in sweat with the dogs at her heels. Their pink tongues lolled out of their mouths, and they gave tired wags rather than their usual exuberant greetings.

"Thank you for taking them out. I really appreciate it." The poor dogs hadn't factored into my day. They were lucky Grace had taken them for a run.

"Finn got away from me. I had to chase him for three blocks." She frowned at him. "You're a bad dog."

He grinned and put more effort into wagging his stubby tail.

"Where's Beau?" It was one thing to forget about the dogs. Forgetting about Beau was unforgivable. Guilt pinched my stomach.

"Bobby's mom took them to the zoo."

"That's right." Relief flooded my veins. "She asked me last week."

"He'll be home for dinner."

"Anarchy and I are having dinner at the club. I thought you could order pizza."

"Aggie promised to make lasagna."

"Even better. After last night—"

"What happened last night?" Libba's eyes narrowed. "Did you try to cook? Because you know how that turns out. Remember that time you caught the kitchen on fire?"

"That's happened more than once," said Grace.

I glowered at the both of them. "Mother served German food."

"Baby cow." Grace's outrage was still evident. "I'm thinking about becoming a vegetarian."

"Wait." Libba held up her free hand. "Frances served foreign food?"

"Yes."

"She's punishing someone."

"Me. She's punishing me."

"None of this is your fault."

"My gun, Libba. I can guarantee you she thinks I should have kept it in a safe."

"What good is a gun in a safe when someone's breaking into your house?"

"That's not the point." Mother didn't care about logic. "Someone used it to kill Prudence."

Grace gasped, and her ruddy cheeks turned pale. "Is that why you asked who I told?"

The last thing I wanted was for Grace to feel like she played any part in this mess.

"I'm sorry."

"Not your fault, honey. Besides, Libba mentioned it to people as well."

"You did?" She gazed at Libba with hope in her eyes.

To her credit, my best friend nodded and lied. "I did. This isn't on you, Grace."

Max ambled over to an air-conditioning vent and collapsed. Finn left us in search of cool bathroom tiles.

Brnng, brnng.

I stared at the phone. I had no doubts as to who was on the other end of the line.

"Are you going to get that?" asked Grace.

"It's Mother."

Libba offered a sympathetic grimace.

Grace reached for the receiver. "Jones' residence." She listened for a moment. "I'm sorry, Granna. She can't come to the phone right now. May I ask her to call you?" Her eyes widened and she nodded. "Yes, ma'am. I'll tell her."

We watched as she returned the receiver to the cradle.

"Granna can be scary."

"True. What did she say?"

"She wants you to call her as soon as you're able. If you don't, she'll come over here, and she guarantees you won't like what happens next."

"I'll call her in a few minutes." The words sounded hollow. I lifted the wine to my lips and sipped.

"What are you doing this weekend, Grace?" Libba earned my eternal gratitude by changing the subject.

"Hanging out with friends. On Sunday, we've got that party at the club. Afterwards, I'm spending the night with Kimberly.

We stay up late watching the Jerry Lewis telethon. It's a tradition."

"I love the telethon. I keep hoping Dean Martin will appear."

I gaped at Libba. There was a better chance that Steele would drop all charges against me than Martin and Lewis having a reunion on live television. The thought was so absurd I almost laughed. Almost.

"I heard Doug Henning is going to be on. I don't want to miss him."

"Well, I heard Frank Sinatra will be on. I used to have such a crush on him." She rolled her eyes. "Your mother preferred Pat Boone."

Grace, who wasn't alive when Frank was a teen idol, shrugged.

The telethon seemed so normal. Somehow, I didn't think I'd be watching.

"I need to shower." Grace headed back toward the kitchen.

"Please tell Aggie about the dinner plans before you head upstairs."

"Sure."

When she was out of earshot, I turned to Libba and whispered, "Thank you."

"For?"

"For telling Grace that you'd told other people where I kept my gun."

"I did that."

"You what?"

"I told people."

"Who?"

"Lord, I don't know. Somebody said that if they found bodies they way you do, they wouldn't be able to sleep at night. I told them you kept a gun in your bedside table."

"So, you told one person. Who?"

"No, Ellison." She swirled her wine. "I told lots of people. I've had some variation on that conversation every time you found a body."

Oh. Good. Lord. I'd found lots of bodies. "We have to tell Hunter."

"Tell him what?"

"That loads of people knew where I kept my gun. It creates reasonable doubt." Maybe they'd drop the charges. Hope bloomed in my chest.

Hope was a dangerous emotion.

"We need more wine." Libba's glass was empty. "I'll grab the bottle."

When she left the room, I picked up the phone and called Mother.

She answered on the third ring. "Walford residence."

"Mother, it's me. I'm returning your call."

"Where have you been?"

"Following leads." I drained my wine glass.

"What's your husband doing?"

"Following other leads."

"Hmph. I've been thinking about who knew where you kept your gun."

"And?"

"The children may have told someone."

I refused to throw poor Grace under the bus. "We've considered that possibility."

"That's as good as a 'yes.' Really, Ellison, the way you baby those children isn't good for them."

"Did you call to critique my parenting?" I offered Libba a grateful smile. She'd returned with the wine bottle and was busy refilling my glass.

"Grace's friend, Mimi Hayes. Did Grace tell her where you kept your gun?"

"I honestly don't know."

"Because Mimi's mother was heard bad-mouthing Prudence two days before she died."

"Who heard her?"

"Everyone at the bridge table." That was interesting.

"What did Georgina say?"

"She said that Prudence was a horrible bi—witch and that no one would be sorry if she died."

Georgina Hayes was a soft-spoken woman. That she'd called Prudence a name was almost unbelievable. "I wonder what Prudence did to bring that on."

"Ask Jinx."

"I will." Although if Jinx knew, she would have mentioned it already.

"Did you learn anything useful, today?"

I thought about the man I'd seen walking into Club K and winced. "Prudence was a blackmailer."

"Despicable," Mother half hissed the word. If she only knew about Henry. "But that's good news. One of her victims probably killed her. Have you told Hunter?"

"Yes. He has a different theory."

"Oh?"

"He thinks someone with a grudge against me is trying to frame me for murder."

Libba, who'd settled on the couch, stared at me with huge, shocked eyes.

"That's…horrible." Mother's voice was taut.

"I agree."

"We'll hope for blackmail."

"Yes, let's do that. Let's hope that Prudence made someone so miserable and desperate that they killed her."

"Ellison Russell!"

"Jones." Why did I bother?

"Whoever killed Prudence should be punished. Prudence

might have been a…" Mother struggled to find an adequate descriptor.

"A horse-toothed harpy," I supplied.

"Yes. That. She may have been a horse-toothed harpy, but she still deserves justice."

"I'm willing to bet that whoever killed her is a better person than she was."

Libba lifted her glass in agreement.

"Doesn't matter," Mother replied. "They murdered another human being, and they should pay for their crime."

I hated it when she was right. "Listen, Mother, Libba is here, and I have to get ready for dinner."

"Dinner? Where are you going?"

"The club. Cricket Hubbell convinced me."

"I always liked that girl. Don't forget to ask Jinx about Georgina Hayes."

"I won't. Goodbye." Feeling relatively unscathed, I hung up the phone.

"Do you think someone's out to get you?" Libba asked.

"I hope not."

"Because, if you're able to beat the wrap—"

"Beat the wrap?"

"Humor me. If you're able to beat the wrap, they may come for you."

"You're just a ray of sunshine."

"I mean it, Ellison. You should be careful."

"I'm always careful."

"Very funny. Whoever this is killed Prudence. Prudence! And if ever there was a woman who was too mean to die, it was her. That means the killer is diabolical."

"They lured her out onto a golf course and shot her."

"With your gun."

I'd somehow become so focused on being a suspect that I'd forgotten a central aspect of Prudence's personality. "The killer must be a man. Prudence would never meet a woman on a golf course after dark."

Libba stared at me from her perch on the edge of the desk and nodded. "You're absolutely right."

Things weren't looking too good for Trip Selden.

CHAPTER ELEVEN

The prickles on the back of my neck were relentless, and the only thing that kept me moving forward was Anarchy's hand on the small of my back. A wave of heat rose from my chest to my face, and I felt a blush crawl across my cheeks. "Everyone's staring," I whispered, my voice barely audible as my heels sank into the carpet.

"Let them," he whispered back.

Cricket and Hubb were already seated at a table in the center of the dining room, which meant I'd have to endure stares from all sides for the entire meal. I felt a sudden, desperate urge to turn around. "We could make a run for it."

"You agreed to this. If it were up to me, we'd be home eating Aggie's lasagna." He increased the pressure of his hand, not to force me forward, but to remind me that he had my back.

"I'm sorry. You can order lasagna here."

"It's not as good."

He was right. And we'd reached the table. It was too late to run.

Hubb stood and kissed my cheek, enveloping me in Paco Rabanne. Then he extended his hand to Anarchy.

"Great dress." Cricket's eyes were warm as she admired my simple Bill Blass sheath.

"You too." Cricket wore a Lilly shift—red and yellow chrysanthemums on a khaki background.

"We're so glad you could join us."

Anarchy pulled out my chair, and I sat. Grateful that I no longer needed to depend on my shaky knees to hold me up. "Us too."

"You'll be at the party on Sunday night?" Cricket asked.

"Yes." I was the hostess. I had to be there. "You?"

"We wouldn't miss it."

Funny, I'd like nothing more than to miss it. A whole night of judgmental stares plus Anne Everist's ire over the lack of vegetables on the kids' buffet? No, thank you. "It should be a fun evening. Is Joey ready to go back to school? A senior, right?"

"Yes. I swear, senior year goes by in a blink." Joey was their youngest. She'd mothered through senior year twice before. "And by the end, between their attitudes and the stress, we'll be ready to shove him out of the nest."

"Where does he want to go to school?"

"Stanford."

"Really? That's Anarchy's alma mater."

"Anarchy," Cricket spoke loud enough to garner my husband's attention, "Ellison just told me you went to Stanford. I don't suppose you'd talk to our son about your experience there?"

"I'd be delighted."

"That's wonderful. Thank you. I had no idea you were an alumnus."

"Nor did I," said Hubb. "What brought you to Kansas City?"

"The police department."

"But you went to Stanford." Cricket sounded confused, as if Stanford and being a police detective were mutually exclusive.

"I always wanted to be a cop."

"But you went to Stanford," she repeated, still struggling to reconcile the concepts.

"Wanting to be a cop didn't mean I didn't also want a good education. Most cops retire around fifty. I figure I'll have a second act."

I stared at my husband, who was just over forty. This was the first I'd heard about an early retirement.

"I'm not cut out to run a bar. Isn't that the expectation? Harrington has been encouraging me to take up golf." He winced and shook his head. "I'm not sure the game is for me. Ellison and I might travel. Who knows? I might start a business."

"What kind of business?" asked Cricket.

Anarchy shrugged. "I have plenty of time to figure it out."

"What about your kiddos, Ellison?" Cricket's smile reached her eyes. "Are they ready for school?"

"We need wide-tip magic markers."

"There's always one thing on the list."

"It's usually rubber cement," I admitted

"You too? I swear, I forgot it for several years running. The art teacher hated me."

"I'm in the same boat."

The small talk was helping. I could almost pretend that half the room wasn't staring at me.

"It must be worse for you. You're an actual artist."

"Who has never, not once, used rubber cement."

Cricket laughed.

"May I get you something to drink, Mrs. Jones?" asked the waiter.

"Club soda with lime and a splash of cranberry, please." I'd had enough alcohol today.

"Mr. Jones?"

"Bourbon. Neat."

The waiter hurried away.

"You're a bourbon drinker?" asked Hubb.

"This week I am." Anarchy sounded absolutely exhausted.

The waiter brought our drinks and took our dinner orders.

We discussed the spacecraft that NASA had sent to Mars and Jack Nicklaus's win at the PGA Championship.

"Mark my words," said Hubb as he tapped the table with his index finger. "Next year is Tom's year." Tom Watson was a popular local golfer who'd made a name for himself on the PGA tour.

"You have some nerve."

I turned as Anarchy and Hubb rose from their chairs.

Sissy MacIntyre stood next to me, her face pinched and hostile. She was an aggressively plain woman—no makeup, dowdy clothes, and a haircut that made her look ten years older than she was. Up until this moment, our interactions had been limited.

"Pardon?" I didn't know what else to say.

"You killed Prudence. You have some nerve showing your face here."

"I did not kill Prudence." I turned my back on her as embarrassment and anger draped around my shoulders like a mink stole.

"Really? The evidence says otherwise. The fight. No alibi. The gun."

"Sissy, you've had too much to drink." Hubb's voice was quiet and firm.

Now that Hubb mentioned it, she did smell of gin.

"She—" Sissy jabbed a finger at me "—is a killer."

"If you touch my wife, I'll have you arrested for assault." Anarchy's low growl seemed to upset her more.

"You!" Now she jabbed at him. "You're as bad as she is. Using your position to help her get away with murder."

"Sissy." My voice was as cold as the ice running through my veins. It was one thing to accuse me of murder, another to accuse my straight-arrow husband of abetting a crime. That was where I drew the line. "Are you familiar with the penalties for slander? I've got a lawyer on retainer, so I'm happy to add a second case."

"You think you're so high and mighty, but you're nothing but a common criminal."

What had I done to her to deserve this level of ire? Was she related to one of the killers I'd helped catch? The thought was terrifying. "I think you should leave."

"You'd like that, wouldn't you? Well, I'm not leaving, not till everyone understands what you've done."

Everyone was staring. Dinners were forgotten in favor of the spectacle. Everyone in the dining room would be burning up the phone lines as soon as they got home. Mother would hear about this within the hour.

Cricket held out her hands. "Sissy, you're making a fool of yourself."

"She. Killed Prudence." Her voice rose with each accusatory word.

I rose. "I did not."

"You need to leave, ma'am. Now." Anarchy's voice brooked no argument.

"You can't tell me what to—"

"Mrs. MacIntyre?" Courtland had joined the circus at our table.

"Courtland." Sissy sounded relieved. She pointed an accusatory finger in my direction. "She shouldn't be here."

"Mrs. Jones is innocent until proven otherwise, and you are making a scene and disturbing the other diners."

She gaped at him. "You're not kicking her out?"

"No, Mrs. MacIntyre, I'm asking you to step out of the dining room."

"B-but…"

"Please, Mrs. MacIntyre." He gestured toward the dining room entrance.

"She killed Prudence!" Her voice was shrill—a final, horrid outburst.

Courtland discreetly took her elbow and guided her out of the crowded room. The man was definitely getting a Christmas bonus. I watched her go, and a profound sense of gratitude washed over me. Anarchy, Hubb, Cricket, and Courtland had stood up for me.

"Ellison, I'm so sorry. I never dreamed anyone would make a scene like that."

I forced a smile as I resumed my seat. "How could you know?"

Anarchy and I exchanged a look. The expression in his eyes said he'd be looking into Sissy MacIntyre first thing in the morning.

"Thank you." I smiled at Hubb and Cricket. "I appreciate your standing up for me."

"Anytime, darling." Cricket reached for my hand and squeezed.

I blinked back tears (they'd been lurking too close to the surface ever since I'd been accused of murder) and faced the dining room with a smile on my face.

WE'D COME HOME TO GRACE ASKING IF A FEW FRIENDS COULD spend the night, and I'd nodded my approval and trudged upstairs.

Now, in the cold, unforgiving light of morning, with an empty Pyrex soaking in the sink, I regretted my decision. Anarchy would not be happy that the girls had devoured Aggie's leftover lasagna like a swarm of locusts.

I gave Mr. Coffee's button a push, and he gurgled at me.

Good morning.

"Is it?" What was good about it?

Rough night?

"I imagine Mother will be storming in here shortly." And if she spotted a dirty dish in the sink, I'd never hear the end of it. Prison might make for a restful reprieve. With a sigh, I turned on the hot water and squeezed dish soap onto a sponge.

What happened?

"A woman I barely know accosted me in the dining room at the club. She loudly insisted I was guilty of murder and insisted I be removed from the premises."

Were you?

"Actually, she was." Again, my heart swelled with gratitude toward Anarchy, Hubb, and Courtland. They'd tried to protect me from her vitriol.

She sounds crazy.

The dogs scratched at the kitchen door, and I let them in. Slightly winded from patrolling the yard for squirrels, rabbits, and cats, they raced to their bowls, gobbled their breakfasts in seconds flat, then looked to me for more. When I shook my head, they hit me with puppy-dog eyes. When that didn't work, they retreated to their beds, collapsing with resigned sighs.

"I don't understand why she went after me like that. I barely know her." A conundrum that had kept me up half the night.

Was she friends with Prudence?

"That seems unlikely. Sissy wears Birkenstocks and clothes she bought in the sixties. No makeup. Long, graying hair. Prudence cared too much about appearances to associate with someone like that." I wondered again if Sissy had a connection to one of the murderers I'd helped catch. If I weren't so certain that Prudence had been on the golf course to meet a man, I'd have suspected Sissy of framing me. She certainly seemed invested in convincing the other club members of my guilt.

I rinsed the Pyrex and grabbed a tea towel.

There's enough for a cup.

"Bless you. Let me put this away." I returned the Pyrex to its cabinet and wiped down the countertops before pouring myself a cup.

After adding cream, I perched on a stool at the island and took my first sip of the day. Things immediately looked brighter. "Just what I needed. Thank you."

My pleasure.

"Mrs. Jones?" One of Grace's friends had made it downstairs without my noticing. Hopefully, she hadn't heard my conversation with Mr. Coffee.

"Mimi, how nice to see you." I hadn't realized she was among the girls spending the night. "What may I get you? The coffee is brewing, or I could make you some tea. We have both orange and cranberry juice."

"No, thank you." She crouched next to Max and scratched behind his ears. His stubby tail thumped a slow rhythm on the floor. "I just came down for a glass of water."

"Of course." I crossed to the cabinet and took a glass from the shelf. "Who else is here?"

"Kimberly, Peggy, Debbie and me."

"A fun crew. Ice?"

"Please."

I reached into the freezer, plunked a few cubes in the glass, and then took a bottle of water from the fridge. "Lemon slice?"

"I'm not that fancy."

"Here you go." I handed her the glass, pretending not to notice the way my hand shook or how the ice clinked in the glass.

"Thank you, Mrs. Jones."

Try as I might, I couldn't think of a tactful way to ask if her mother had murdered Prudence, so I let her return upstairs without mentioning homicide.

Nice girl.

"Her mother may have killed Prudence. It's also possible that her father is the killer. They might be in on it together. And if she stole my gun, she's an accessory."

That sweet girl?

"Her mother had a beef with Prudence, and Mimi knew where I kept my gun."

Mr. Coffee did not look convinced.

I resumed my perch on my stool, resting my elbows on the island and staring at nothing. "It's not enough for the prosecutor to drop the charges. Unless the real killer is caught, I'll be tainted. Grace will be tainted. Beau will be tainted."

Not Anarchy?

"Him too. It won't help his career if people think his wife got away with murder."

What if you're acquitted?

I couldn't be acquitted without first going to trial. A possibility that curdled the coffee in my stomach. "Not good enough. There would still be talk. We have to catch the killer, and if catching him means I suspect everyone I know, so be it."

Brnng, brnng.

The phone's ringer seemed unnaturally loud in the quiet of an early Saturday. It could only be one person. Reluctantly, I stood and picked up the receiver. "Jones' residence."

"What happened last night?" Mother demanded.

"You heard."

"I heard that a crazy woman started yelling at you in the dining room at the club and that you behaved admirably."

I was pushing middle-age, but Mother's rare praise still had the ability to lift my spirits. "Sissy MacIntyre."

"I went to grade school with her father. I'm not surprised his daughter is a loon."

"It was awful."

"I'm sure it was. If I'd been there…well, I heard Anarchy and Hubb took up for you." She sounded approving.

I swirled the coffee in my mug and waited for the axe to fall. Mother never called to say nice things.

"Ask Hunter about getting a restraining order."

My knee-jerk reaction was to tell her I didn't need one, to argue, but I let the idea sit for a few seconds before responding. "That's not a bad idea. When I speak with him, I'll mention it."

"Is there anything I can do to help?"

When I was in high school, a date took me to see *Invasion of the Body Snatchers*. The movie scared the pants off me, but I thought of it now. Had an empathetic alien snatched Mother's body? "Thank you for offering. We can't forget Fob."

"Who?" The confused frown on Mother's face was evident in her voice.

"Married man. Prudence claimed he was leaving his wife for her."

Mother tsked. "If ever a woman was misnamed, it was Prudence Davies. Her mother should have named her Jezebel."

"She did get around."

Mother laughed. Laughed! "That's putting it mildly. I'll keep my ear peeled for Fob."

"Thank you."

"You're welcome. I'll talk to you soon." She hung up, and I stared at the receiver in my hand.

What's wrong?

"Mother was pleasant." I returned the receiver to its cradle and refilled my mug, wincing as a herd of elephants careened down the backstairs.

Five teenage girls spilled into the kitchen, their smiles and laughter jarring.

"Good morning." I waved at them from my perch.

"Good morning, Mrs. Jones." They'd all gotten it right. That deserved a reward.

I roused myself to stand. And smile. "Who'd like breakfast? I can make pancakes."

As one, they edged toward the door, their expressions a mix of polite regret and barely disguised horror.

"Gosh, that sounds great," said Peggy. "But we've got to get to—"

"To practice," Kimberly blurted.

"For what?" I asked.

They exchanged panicked looks, a silent conversation passing between them.

Watching them try to formulate a lie on the spot was entertaining.

"Cheer. It's cheer practice."

"Funny, Grace didn't say anything about that."

"Because she's so good. The rest of us need extra practice time."

"I see." I covered my lips to hide their amused twitch. "Are you sure you have practice on a holiday weekend?"

"No. But if we do, we don't want to miss it." They rushed out the backdoor, leaving me with Grace.

"You know how to clear a room."

"My cooking isn't that bad."

"Sorry, but it is." She opened the fridge, took out a bottle of orange juice, and poured herself a glass.

"Did you have fun last night?"

"Kimberly's mom almost didn't let her come."

Her best friend's mother worried about letting her daughter come to our house. I hated that being charged with murder was causing Grace trouble. We had to catch the killer. Quickly. "I'm sorry."

She rolled her eyes. "It's not your fault."

"If it weren't for that gun…"

Grace's eyes met mine. "Every girl who spent the night last night told her mother that you kept a gun in your nightstand."

I wondered how that had come up. "I just can't imagine any of those women sneaking through our house to steal it."

Georgina Hayes dressed up like a cartoon cat-burglar—black pants, black sweater, black stocking cap (despite the heat), and a black mask that tied at the back of her head? The idea was ridiculous. Except someone had done exactly that. Although they'd probably eschewed the stereotypical clothes.

"Mom, we have to figure this out."

"I know, sweetheart. We're trying."

CHAPTER TWELVE

W hen I returned to the kitchen an hour later, dressed in shorts, a T-shirt, and running shoes, and ready to take the dogs out, I found Aggie with her head in the fridge.

She turned when my sneakers squeaked against the floor. "What happened to the lasagna?"

"Grace had friends spend the night. They polished it off."

She frowned. "Did Detective Jones get any?"

"No." Anarchy had left early for the station, giving me a quick kiss and promising to find out everything there was to know about Sissy MacIntyre. Lasagna had been the last thing on his mind.

"I'll make another. It's his favorite."

"Thank you."

I lifted the dogs' leashes off their hooks, and then Max and Finn danced around my legs, their nails clicking like mad. The expressions on their doggy faces, sheer unadulterated joy, lightened my heart.

"How far are you going?"

"A couple of times around the park. Why?"

"In case Mrs. Walford calls."

"Ah. I've already spoken to her today. She was in…a good mood."

Aggie tilted her head and frowned as if I'd suddenly switched from English to Swahili. I understood her confusion. Mother didn't do good moods.

"Amazing, right?" I hooked the worn leather leashes to collars and headed toward the door.

"Have a good run."

We walked the first two blocks, the sidewalk already radiating the morning's heat. Thick, humid air clung to my skin. Somewhere, the next block over, a lawnmower roared to life.

I increased our pace to a steady jog. Fast enough to engage the dogs, slow enough to allow me to think.

We ran, and I made lists. To do: wide-tip magic markers, Grace's shampoo, call Darla Higgins, catch a killer.

We ran, and I reviewed every second of my fight with Prudence. Had she said anything that might lead me to her killer?

We ran, and I began a list of people who might want her dead. It was too long. I needed a pad of paper.

We ran, and I imagined life in prison. Bad idea. My lungs lost their ability to process air.

Two laps around the park left me with wringing wet hair, clothes plastered to my damp body, and the leash handles slick with sweat from my hands. I'd had enough. "Let's head for home, guys."

Finn pulled on his leash, not ready to leave.

"Buddy, it's hot out here." Huge understatement.

His pink tongue hung out of his mouth, and he panted like he'd never get another chance, but he still refused to budge.

"Finn." I tried to sound stern. "We're going home."

With poor grace, he followed me across the street.

Max, who'd been easy, lunged at a squirrel, nearly toppling me.

Finn took advantage of my break in attention and lunged the other way. I lost my hold on his leash, and the Airedale ran away.

"Finn! Come back here."

He ignored me.

Max and I followed. Sort of. A loose dog was much faster than a human. Especially a human trying to keep a Weimaraner under some semblance of control.

"Finn!" Yelling wasn't helping. If anything, my voice made him run faster.

A block from the park, he treed a squirrel, standing at the bottom of the oak to stare into its branches, where the squirrel chittered angrily. I tiptoed within a few feet of his dangling leash and leaped.

Grass-stained knees became part of my ensemble, and Finn ran again.

I hauled myself off the ground. "Finn!"

He stopped, stared at me, and for a brief second, I thought he might actually listen. "Come."

He tore around the side of a house, disappearing into some-one's backyard.

I had no choice but to follow.

Max and I jogged up the driveway. Max was panting hard, while I swore softly.

I rounded the corner of the house and stopped dead in my tracks. Finn was nowhere in sight. What was very much evident were two men locked in a passionate embrace.

Without a word, I dragged Max back down the driveway. Only when I reached the sidewalk did I bellow, "Finn!"

My errant dog came racing toward me from a different back-yard, and I lunged for his leash. That I actually caught the worn leather strap was pure luck. "You are a bad dog."

He wagged his tail and grinned.

I glanced at the house whose backyard I'd invaded, a stately

Tudor, and rubbed my eyes. Obviously, I needed them checked. I was being silly. It wasn't as if I'd seen actual faces (the faces had been mashed together). And many men were tall and lanky. There was no way—no way—I'd just seen Hubb kissing another man.

"Come on." I yanked at Finn's leash. "We're going home."

Walking into the cold bite of the air-conditioning was heavenly. I paused just past the doorway and let the chill kiss my overheated skin.

The dogs slurped down copious amounts of water before collapsing on the cool floor.

"You're back." Aggie walked into the kitchen carrying a basket of laundry.

"Finn got away."

His stubby tail thumped against the floor. He knew we were talking about him.

She eyed my green knees and winced. "Do you need an antiseptic?"

"I'm fine." I opened the fridge, took out the water bottle, and filled a glass, drinking thirstily. Only when the glass was empty did I ask, "Any calls?"

"Not a one." Aggie's surprise was evident.

"Something is up with Mother." And if it left her in a pleasant mood, I was all for it.

"What are your plans for the day?"

I considered my to-do list. Three out of four items were easily achievable. "Errands and calls. You?"

"I'm almost caught up with the laundry. When I get the last load in, I'll head to the market. I thought I'd roast a chicken." She smiled. "And make another lasagna."

Aware that I smelled worse than roadkill, I kept my response short. "Yum." Then I headed upstairs to shower."

When I sat down at my desk to call Darla, I felt like a new woman. Or at least I smelled like one. I'd even spritzed Rive

Gauche on my pulse points. I felt clean, confident, and ready for the rest of my day. The iced coffee that Aggie had made for me didn't hurt either.

I took a sip and dialed.

"Hello."

"Hello, may I please speak with Darla Higgins?"

"This is she."

"Darla, it's Ellison Jones on the line."

"You called back." She sounded surprised.

"I'm sorry it took so long. I've got a lot going on." Huge understatement. "Are you available to swing by the bank next week? How about Wednesday?"

"Yes. Of course. Wednesday is great. I wanted to thank you."

"For?"

"Sending me your lawyer. He got all the charges dropped."

"He's very good at his job."

"What about you? Still facing a murder charge?"

"I'm afraid so."

"I bet Mr. Tafft can fix it."

"Here's hoping. Does ten o'clock suit you?"

"Yes! Ten o'clock next Wednesday. I'll be there. And, for what it's worth, I know you're innocent. You're good people. Good people aren't killers."

"Thank you." Sadly, Darla was wrong. Given the right circumstances, good people did commit murder. "I'll see you Wednesday."

We hung up, and I called Jinx.

She answered on the third ring. "Hello."

"It's me. Ellison."

"I heard you had quite a night."

"Any idea why Sissy MacIntyre wants me in jail?"

"She had aspirations of being a painter. It didn't work out. Now she hand paints tooled-leather belts and handbags and sells them at craft fairs."

That sounded awful. "What does her husband do?"

"He's gone. Passed away a couple of years ago. But it's not her husband's money that lets her paint daisies on coin purses. The real money in that marriage came from her family."

"She was…unhinged."

"Maybe she's jealous." Jinx's suggestion was entirely reasonable, but it seemed off to me. There had to be another reason.

"Any idea what Prudence did to make Georgina Hayes so angry?"

"No, drat the luck. No one seems to know."

Which meant I'd have to find out myself. "Say, do you know who lives at 824 West 53rd Street?" It was the house whose backyard I'd invaded.

"I don't. Doesn't Anne Everist live on that block?"

"You might be right. I'll ask her when I see her tomorrow night." Assuming she was speaking to me after Courtland and I vetoed having cooked vegetables on the kids' buffet. I could almost hear her—*I wanted healthy options, but Ellison wouldn't allow it. Did you know she was arrested for murder?*

"Ellison, I picked up the phone on my way out the door. Can I talk to you later?"

"I'll see you at the party."

"Sounds like a plan. Bye."

I hung up the phone, took a sip of my coffee, and planned the rest of my day. First stop: the drugstore in the Village.

WHEN J.C. NICHOLS DECIDED TO CREATE A NEW CITY, JUST across the state line from Kansas City, he chose to name it after Prairie School, which already enjoyed a rich history. I had no idea why he chose to call his new city a village. Maybe he thought it sounded quaint. At any rate, Prairie Village, Kansas was created. At its center was a shopping center, and in that shopping center was a drugstore that sold highly elusive chamomile shampoo. It was Grace's favorite. She claimed it made the gold highlights in her hair shine like nobody's business.

Which is why I found myself parked in front of Tiffany Town. I resisted the store's siren call (I didn't need greeting cards, or wrapping paper, or cute little pads of paper held together with grosgrain bows) and walked down the mall to the drugstore where I bought every bottle of chamomile shampoo they had in stock.

"Will there be anything else for you, Mrs. Russell?"

"It's Jones, now."

The white-haired lady behind the counter blushed. "I apologize. It's just that you were Mrs. Russell for such a long time."

"It's fine." I handed over an obscene amount of money for four bottles of shampoo and pocketed a few coins as change.

I was on my way out when someone called my name. "Ellison!"

I turned, spotted Betty Brewster, and forced a smile. I wasn't in the mood for probing questions about murder.

"How are you?" Betty was a porcelain-doll of a woman. Petite. Blonde. Her blue eyes had always struck me as vacant. "It's been ages since I've seen you."

"Fine, thank you. I see Pam at the pool. She saved a little girl's life."

"That's what Fred told me. He said he heard it from you. Such a roundabout way to learn of my daughter's heroics." Her hands fluttered like butterflies trapped in a net, and she blinked rapidly.

I saw actual tears in her eyes. "Sometimes daughters aren't the best at sharing." Although, if Grace saved a child, I was fairly certain she'd tell me about it. Then she'd demand her favorite meal, a shopping spree, and an extension of her curfew.

"Pam says I make too much of a fuss." A single tear escaped, and she quickly wiped it off her cheek. "Tell me, how is Grace?"

"Wonderful. Excited for school to start."

"Someone told me you're adopting a little boy."

"That's right. His name is Beau." Lord only knew what social services would do if they learned I'd been accused of murder. The mere thought made my blood run cold. I'd have to ask Hunter what we needed to do.

"How lovely. You'll have someone in the house even after Grace is gone." She wiped another tear, her gaze shifting to the floor.

"Betty, are you all right?"

Her chin wobbled. "Just sad. I hate it when Pam goes back to Lawrence. Fred works so much, and I'm often alone at night."

The cynical, he-done-her-wrong side of me couldn't help but wonder if something other than work kept Fred away from home. Betty seemed…needy. And, in my limited experience, most men didn't like needy women. "When does Pam go back to school?"

"Monday. We moved her into her apartment last weekend, so all she has to do is show up for class on Tuesday." She gave me a watery smile, her gaze not quite meeting mine. "Has Grace started her college search? Fred wanted Pam to go back east, but it's nice having her so close."

"I'm sure it is."

"The poor girl. She's been so upset, what with a body being found on the golf course." She pressed her hands to her chest as if she too was upset by Prudence's demise. "I hope Pam will settle when she gets back to school."

Did Betty not know I'd been arrested for Prudence's murder? If so, she might be the only person of my acquaintance who wasn't whispering about it. I knew some of those whispers were in support, but they were still whispers. "I hope so, too." I held up my bag of shampoo. "This is just one stop of many—"

"What did you buy?"

"Shampoo for Grace."

"I stopped by to pick up my prescription." She looked over her shoulder at the line in front of the pharmacy counter. "Then I'm off to Tiffany Town. Fred likes those monogrammed pads for his office." She wrinkled her nose. "I'm afraid he uses them as stationery."

"At least he writes personal notes."

"I suppose there is that. It was lovely to see you."

"Likewise."

I was tempted to dash into The Jones' Store, their designer department was rather fabulous, but the thought of running into Betty at Tiffany Town had me hurrying to my car. Really, I couldn't leave fast enough.

CHAPTER THIRTEEN

I arrived home with a package of wide-tip magic markers, four bottles of shampoo, and the start of a headache throbbing behind my eyes.

Beau and the dogs met me at the door, whirlwinds of inexhaustible energy.

"Markers." I handed Beau the package. "You should put them with the rest of your school supplies."

He nodded but didn't move, regarding me with eyes that seemed too big for his face. "Can we talk?"

My stomach clenched. I knew what this was about, and guilt twisted like a knife in my gut. We should have talked to him before now, before he heard a rumor. "Do you mind if I pour myself an Arnold Palmer?" I needed a moment to think about what I should tell him.

"Nope." He followed me into the kitchen, and the dogs trailed after him.

I added ice to a glass and took a bottle from the fridge, pouring the perfect amount of lemonade over the ice. Then I added tea from the pitcher on the counter. "Want anything, Beau?"

"No, thank you." His voice was small.

I perched on a stool and prepared to fail—there was no way I could give him all the answers he needed. "What's on your mind?"

He settled on the floor next to Finn and ran his fingers over the dog's short, wiry coat. The motion seemed to soothe him. Long seconds passed before he said, "Bobby's mom told him you might go to prison."

My heart stuttered at the pain in his voice, and I searched for the right words. There had to be something I could say that would wipe away the pain and worry I heard in his voice. "I've been accused of a crime." My voice was as calm as I could make it. "I'm innocent. Anarchy and Mr. Tafft are doing everything they can to prove I didn't do it."

"Kill Ms. Davies, you mean?" His gaze finally lifted, meeting mine. His eyes were wide and scared.

Just how much had Bobby's mother told him? That self-righteous, interfering, holier-than-thou woman deserved a punch to the throat. I slipped off the stool and joined him on the floor, sitting cross-legged next to him. "That's right."

He nodded, working his lower lip with his teeth as he drew his knees up to his chin. "What will happen if Anarchy can't prove you didn't do it?"

I tilted my head toward the ceiling and exhaled. "I suppose there will be a trial, and then a jury will decide that I didn't kill Ms. Davies." Just the thought of a trial made my incipient headache ten times worse.

Beau, whose fingers still stroked the dog's coppery coat, swallowed loudly. "What if the jury thinks you did it—" his voice cracked, and he took a few seconds to collect himself. "What if they decide you killed Ms. Davies?"

"They won't. I'm not going anywhere, Beau. I promise." Grace was used to the craziness at our house—the bodies, the people who tried to kill me, the worry—and somewhere along the line, she'd decided that, no matter what, things would turn out okay. Beau didn't have that certainty. Some days, I didn't either.

"Why do people have to be so mean?" he whispered.

I smoothed a lock of hair away from his brow as my heart broke. Beau had been through so much in his short life. Now this. I hated that Prudence's murder was cracking the foundation of his life with us. "I wish I knew. I do know this—not everyone is mean. There are good people. People who will love you and protect you and cherish you."

He swiped angrily at his cheek. "I don't want you to go away."

My jaw ached with the sudden need to cry. I swallowed hard and wrapped my arm around his shoulders. "Not happening. You're stuck with me. No matter what, I'll be here for you." That was a promise I'd move mountains to keep.

"Ellison?" Anarchy's voice boomed from the front hall, loud enough to make the dogs jump to their paws. Max even barked.

"We're in the kitchen," I called.

He burst into the room, his face alight with hope, and swept me off the floor and into his arms. Then he swung me in a giddy circle.

"What happened?" I was almost breathless with relief. The news had to be exculpatory. After all, my steady husband wasn't given to dizzying displays of emotion. "Did Morrison find the real killer?"

"No." He let my feet touch the ground but kept his tight hold on me.

"Then what?" The disappointment was almost tangible. I wasn't cleared. Not yet.

"Peters showed me a copy of the report on your gun. There were unidentified prints on the grip."

That was it? The joy. The spinning. For fingerprints? I'd hoped for more. Unless the new prints were on file... "Whose?"

"We're not sure. It doesn't matter. Those prints create reasonable doubt."

Reasonable doubt wasn't good enough. An acquittal wasn't good enough. Not for me. Not for my husband. Not for my children. The police had to arrest the real killer.

"Does this mean it's over?" Beau sounded so hopeful—so terribly, terribly hopeful. He pressed his hands together as if he were praying.

"Not quite." Anarchy relaxed his hold on me, bent, and ruffled Beau's hair. "But the police will have to look for whoever left those prints. If Morrison hadn't been in such a hurry, if he'd waited for the report, he might not have made an arrest. The prosecutor would never have filed charges with what they have now."

"Will Steele drop the charges?" It was a silly question. Steele wouldn't drop the charges. Not if he thought there was a chance he might put me in prison. I'd seen the naked ambition on the man's face. He wanted to make a name for himself.

"We should call Hunter. Right away." There was a lightness in Anarchy's voice I hadn't heard in days. He'd been more worried than he'd admitted. "I'll call him. I just had to tell you first." He kissed my forehead and squeezed me against his chest.

I smiled up at him and didn't say what I was thinking. Dropping the charges wasn't good enough. Until the police arrested someone else, I'd live under a cloud of suspicion. "Tell Peters 'Thank you.'" Anarchy's irascible partner wasn't exactly my biggest fan. I strongly suspected he'd shared information that Morrison wanted kept quiet. I also suspected he'd done it for Anarchy's benefit, not mine.

"I'll tell him."

"If I give you an address, can you find out who owns the house?"

"Sure. Why?"

"I saw something this morning, and it's bothering me."

"Does it pertain to your case?"

"It might."

"What's the address?"

"West 53rd Street. The house number is 824."

He nodded. "I'll have an answer for you in a few minutes. First, I want to call Hunter." He swiped a sip of my Arnold Palmer and practically bounced out of the kitchen on his way to his study.

That left me, Beau, and the dogs.

Beau regarded me with serious eyes and rose to his feet. "You're not as happy as Anarchy. Why not?"

"I want everyone to know I'm innocent."

Max whined softly and pressed against me.

Beau frowned. "I know you're innocent. So do Grace and Anarchy and Aggie and Libba and Charlie and—"

"Come here."

He stepped into my open arms—the sweetest little boy on the planet. I hugged him tightly. "Thank you, Beau."

"For what?"

"For reminding me who matters." But I still wanted the killer charged, tried, and convicted. That was the only way my name would ever be fully cleared.

Woof!

The dogs sprang forward, their nails clicking on the floor as they struggled for purchase. Half a second later, they careened out of the kitchen, racing toward the front door, and the man who dared push paper through the slot every day.

Woof! Woof! Woof!

Max had never cared about the postman until Finn moved in. Now, barking at the poor man was his job. A job he took seriously.

"I'd better get the mail before they shred it." I hurried into the front hall, collecting already scattered envelopes as the dogs pressed their noses against the glass panels that flanked the door.

"Ellison." Anarchy stood in the doorway to his study. "I have an answer for you."

"That was fast."

"Hunter's out of the office. Georgina and Malcolm Hayes own the house on 53rd Street."

I dropped the salvaged mail on the bombé chest in the foyer. "That can't be right. They live on Stratford Road." I'd picked up and dropped off Mimi at their Georgian home more times than I could count.

"Not according to the county records."

"Maybe they moved." It was possible. I hadn't driven any of Grace's friends since she got her license, and if the Hayes family moved close to one of the many times I'd found a body, I might have missed it.

"Why are you interested in that house?"

I glanced toward the kitchen and lowered my voice. "Finn got away from me at Loose Park. He ran into the backyard. I followed him and saw two men kissing."

Anarchy leaned against the doorframe, crossed his ankles, and cocked a brow, waiting for more.

"I thought one of the men was Hubb." I glanced at the oriental beneath my feet, then forced myself to meet his gaze. "It's just that Cricket and Hubb have been unusually friendly since I was arrested." I hated the suspicious turn my mind had taken, but it wasn't unheard of for murderers to cozy up to the investigations of their crimes.

"You think Prudence might have blackmailed Hubb."

"Or Malcolm. Either way, they'd want to know if Morrison found anything."

"Are you sure it was Hubb?"

"I didn't see a face."

"But?"

"The clothes, the body type, the hair—they were all his." I pressed my fingertips against my temples, pushing back the pain from my headache. "Also, Georgina and Malcolm's daughter is friends with Grace. Mimi knew where I kept my gun."

"Invite them for cocktails."

I blinked rapidly. "What?"

"Invite them. Tonight. You can invite Libba and Charlie and Liz and Perry, so it doesn't look too obvious."

My headache amped up another level. "Why are we inviting them?"

"Because we'll be able to lift prints from their glasses."

"Can we do that?"

He quirked a brow.

I wasn't questioning his ability to lift a print. "Would the prints be admissible?"

"Yes."

I shook my head, which did terrible things to the pain lurking behind my eyes. "It feels like trickery."

He tilted his chin. "How badly do you want to be cleared of murder charges?"

"I'll make the calls."

LIBBA BREEZED THROUGH MY FRONT DOOR AT PRECISELY FIVE o'clock and announced, "I need a martini."

I needed three. "We've already got a pitcher made just for you. Where's Charlie?"

"He'll be here shortly. He got held up with a patient." She glanced around the foyer. "Where's my martini?"

"Right here." Anarchy stepped out of the living room and handed her a glass.

She sipped and sighed. "Strong and dirty, just the way I like it."

I rolled my eyes at her.

"What's the occasion?" she asked.

"What do you mean?" Somehow, I didn't want to admit—not even to Libba—that I'd invited my friends so that we could surreptitiously collect their husbands' fingerprints.

"You don't host impromptu cocktail parties. I'm hoping I'm here because you got good news."

"Nope. Just needed some cheering up."

Her expression softened, and she reached for my hand. "We'll get through this."

I sure hoped so. "Looks like the Hubbells are here." I'd spotted Cricket and Hubb through the glass panels flanking the front door.

Libba released my fingers, and I donned a welcoming smile and reached for the door handle. "Come in, come in. It's hotter than the hinges of hell out there."

A second later, Cricket and Hubb were in my foyer, and we were exchanging air kisses as I held my breath against the onslaught of Paco Rabanne.

I stepped away from Hubb's embrace, refilled my lungs, and said, "Aggie made some hors d'oeuvres." Aggie had risen to the challenge of an impromptu cocktail party. Silver trays on the coffee table display cheese puffs, a chutney cheesecake surrounded by a variety of crackers, baba ghanoush with wedges of toasted pita bread, and an array of fresh vegetables served with French onion dip.

"Wow, Ellison. This looks delicious. When I host cocktails, my guests are lucky to get a cheeseball. Hubb, honey, we won't need dinner."

"Cricket, what may I get you to drink?" Anarchy stood by the bar cart, ready to pour. "Hubb, bourbon?"

Cricket asked for white wine, and Hubb eagerly accepted an old-fashioned glass with two fingers of Old Grand-Dad.

Ding dong.

"Excuse me." I returned to the foyer and opened the front door to Liz and Perry and Georgina and Malcolm.

More air kisses were exchanged.

"Ellison, I'm so glad you called. Malcolm and I had nothing going on tonight. This is such fun!"

"She's right," said Liz. "We're thrilled you called." Liz was an extrovert. Nights spent at home were an anathema to her.

"I'm just thrilled you could all join us. Drinks and nibbles in the living room."

Liz held back as her husband and Georgina and Malcolm walked in front of us, stopping me with a hand on my arm. "How are you?"

"I've been better. This helps. Having friends around." Especially friends I didn't suspect were letting me take the fall for a murder they'd committed.

She gave me a quick hug, and we headed to the living room, where Anarchy was already holding out two gin and tonics—one for Georgina, one for Malcolm.

"Liz, what can I get you?" Anarchy asked as he poured bourbon over ice for Perry.

"A vodka soda, please. Two limes."

"Done. Ellison?"

"White wine," I replied.

Cricket took a seat on the couch next to Libba. "I heard the loveliest rumor."

"Oh?" Libba lifted her left eyebrow.

"I heard that you and Charlie are getting married."

Libba flushed. "Not exactly. There are issues."

"With Charlie?"

"Heavens, no. Charlie's perfect. With me."

Cricket tilted her head, waiting for more.

"There are things I haven't told him. Things I need to tell him." Her tone made it clear she'd rather slide down a razor blade into a pool of rubbing alcohol.

I frowned. Libba was my oldest friend, and I knew all her

secrets. Not a single one would keep Charlie from making her his wife.

Cricket patted Libba's tanned knee. "Oh, honey. There isn't a marriage out there without secrets."

"This is a big secret."

My frown deepened. What big secret?

Cricket dismissed Libba's objection with a flick of her wrist. "I stand by my statement."

"What are you girls talking about over there?" called Georgina.

"The things we don't tell our husbands."

She took a large sip of her drink. "What about the secrets our husbands don't tell us?"

Cricket's lips curled into a knowing smile. "Now those secrets are probably grounds for blackmail."

Malcolm dropped his glass, jumping away from the splash. "Dammit. Ellison, I'm so sorry."

"Don't give it a second thought. That's the beauty of clear liquors. They don't stain." I knelt and picked his glass off the carpet. "I'll grab a towel, and Anarchy will make you a fresh drink." Trying my best to avoid the center of the glass, where Malcolm's fingerprints were probably the clearest, I carried the glass to the kitchen and slipped it into a plastic storage bag. Then I hid the bag in the pantry and grabbed a tea towel.

One set down, one to go.

CHAPTER FOURTEEN

I rested my cheek against Anarchy's chest; its steady rise and fall comforted me.

He traced lazy circles on my bare shoulder.

The hum of the overhead fan in our bedroom created a soothing white noise.

I snuggled closer, letting Anarchy's clean, manly scent wrap me in a sense of safety. When we were together like this, I almost believed everything would work out.

Anarchy yawned. The poor man was exhausted. We should have been in bed hours ago, but our friends had stayed late, drinking countless cocktails and making a meal of Aggie's delicious hors d'oeuvres.

"What happens next?" I hated disturbing our serenity, but I needed to know.

"I'll take all three glasses to the lab in the morning."

I stiffened. "Three?"

Anarchy traced another circle. "Malcolm, Hubb, and Georgina."

"Georgina?" I already felt lower than low for collecting

Malcolm and Hubb's prints. With Georgina's, I was officially betraying a friend.

"When was the last time their daughter was over here?"

"Mimi? Before the most recent sleepover, I honestly couldn't tell you." Grace and Mimi had been inseparable in middle school. But they'd grown apart in their freshman year of high school. While they remained on good terms, Grace's best friends were now Debbie, Peggy, and Kimberly.

"We need to ask Grace."

I laid my hand on his very solid chest, feeling the steady beat of his heart beneath my palm. "Let's wait until we get the prints back before saying anything to Grace. There's no reason to make her start doubting her friends." No reason to make her feel guilty about betraying them. "Not unless the prints on the gun belong to Georgina or Malcolm."

"Agreed. Did you notice, Malcolm dropped his drink when Cricket mentioned blackmail?"

"I noticed. It might have been a coincidence." I didn't believe that for a second.

"No such thing."

There absolutely were coincidences, but that was a discussion for another day. "We're assuming Prudence blackmailed Malcolm. So, he decided to kill her, stole my gun, lured her to the golf course, and shot her?" Spoken aloud, the theory sounded barely plausible. But someone had done exactly that.

"It could have been Hubb." His hand gently cupped my cheek, his touch no more than a whisper.

"Why my gun? Either one of those men could buy a weapon. It's not as if the ballistics for new guns are on file."

"Maybe time was of the essence."

"But the risk," I argued. "What would he say if he were discovered on the second floor of our home, pawing through my drawers?"

"What would anyone say?"

"If it were a woman, she'd say she came to see me. When she arrived, she found the house unlocked, and when I didn't answer her call, she got worried and decided to search and make sure I was okay."

"That takes us back to Georgina."

"I can't picture Prudence meeting a woman on the golf course."

"I can't picture a blackmailer agreeing to meet one of their victims in a remote location in the middle of the night." He made a good point.

Why had Prudence gone to the golf course? "So, we're nowhere."

"Not exactly. We have the prints. If one of them matches, your case just got a million times stronger." His fingers traced the line of my jaw, and butterflies took flight in my stomach. "There's absolutely no reason anyone else's prints should be on your gun unless they stole it."

"I know matching the prints might clear me, but it feels wrong to hope that one of my friends committed murder." I closed my eyes for a few seconds and voiced my latest fear. "What if none of the prints match?"

"Then we keep looking. I'm not giving up, Ellison." He pulled me closer, the tiny space between us vanishing entirely, and ghosted a kiss across my lips.

"Is the lab even working this weekend?"

"Of course."

"I'm sure they're understaffed for the holiday. And it's not as if these prints are a priority for anyone but us." Although they could be. I put that thought right out of my head. Prudence might have been a blackmailer. I was not.

"I have that covered."

"Oh?" I tipped my head back and caught the glimmer in his brown eyes.

"People will do almost anything for Aggie's chocolate Bundt cake."

"A bribe, Detective Jones?" I teased.

"I prefer the word 'incentive.'" He kissed me again. Slowly. Thoroughly. Like we had all night. "We'll get this figured out," he murmured against my mouth. "If the prints come back, Morrison will have to expand the investigation, and Steele will have to drop the charges. If they don't, we're no worse off than we were before."

I wanted to believe him. I wanted to *hope*. But what if he was wrong? What if we were still poised on the edge of disaster?

He kissed me again, and I wished I could drown in the press of his lips against mine, forget the world, and do nothing but feel. But I couldn't. Worry still wrapped around my neck like a noose, and what Cricket and Georgina had said about secrets weighed too heavily on my conscience. Anarchy already knew about my lunch with Nancy. What I hadn't told him was that I'd gone to Club K afterwards. "There's something I have to tell you."

He pulled his lips away. "Nothing good ever follows that sentence."

"It's not *bad*. Per se." Long seconds passed as I searched for the best way to tell him.

"Rip off the Band-Aid, Ellison."

"I went to Club K." The words tumbled on top of each other.

His body went rigid. "When? Why?"

"Prudence was blackmailing Nancy because she saw her at Club K. I wondered if Prudence had identified anyone else with deep pockets."

"Had she?"

"Yes. Trip Selden. He's a prominent attorney."

"Married?"

"With five children. One of whom, Courtney, is friendly with Grace. Not that being friends with Grace means she knew about the gun." But it increased the odds. Frustration bubbled in my chest. "The longer this goes on, the more I think half of Kansas City knew where I kept my gun."

"We should have asked him for cocktails."

I couldn't tell if he was joking.

"Wait. Is his wife's name Lucia?"

I frowned. "How did you know?"

"She was on Courtland's list of people with grudges against Prudence."

Interesting. But I needed to tell him everything before we discussed Lucia and Trip. "That's not all."

"Oh?"

"When I was leaving Club K, I saw someone else. Someone Prudence might not have known about. Kathleen said he was a private client."

"Who?" Anarchy gave me a moment to answer; when I didn't, he repeated, "Band-Aid, Ellison."

"Judge Caldwell." Barely a whisper.

He let out a long, slow breath. "Well...damn."

"I know."

"If he killed Prudence, he's in the perfect position to make sure a scapegoat is found guilty."

The thought had occurred to me, gnawed at me, terrified me. "How would he get my gun?" That was the question I couldn't get over, the question that gave me a semblance of hope.

"We just decided half the town knew where you kept it."

"Half the middle-aged town. Half the teenaged town. Not half the gray-haired town."

"Judge Caldwell and Mistress K." He shook his head. "Does anyone in this town have a healthy, monogamous relationship?"

"Us."

He chuckled and brushed a kiss across my forehead. "Why didn't you tell me you were going to Club K?"

I heard an edge in his voice and chose my words carefully. "You were working, and I was only a few minutes away from the club when I decided to go." I adored Anarchy with every fiber of my being, but I was done justifying my actions to men (even the one I loved). If my explanation wasn't enough, we had a problem. "I *can* take care of myself."

"I know you can. I just hate thinking of you there alone. I hate thinking of you there at all."

"You do remember I own the building?"

"How could I forget?" His finger traced another circle on my shoulder, and I melted into his chest. "Judge Caldwell."

"Should we tell Hunter?"

He grunted, clearly not thrilled about sharing.

"Got a better idea?"

"Sadly, no. Do you want me to call him in the morning?"

"I'll do it. You're going to the lab."

"Tell me more about Trip Selden."

"He's always seemed like a nice man—well, nice for an attorney. He and Henry were friends." Not exactly a glowing recommendation. "He wears Paco Rabanne Pour Homme."

Anarchy groaned. "Another one?"

"It's the expensive cologne of the moment." Then, pronouncing each syllable carefully and using a fake Brahmin accent, I added, "No English Leather or Old Spice allowed at the club, darling."

He drew me closer until the lengths of our bodies pressed together. "Is that so?"

"Mhmm."

"I have a bottle of English Leather."

I buried my nose in his neck and inhaled. "Do you? I prefer you without cologne."

"Do you?"

I kissed his jaw. A line of tiny kisses that ended at his chin. "Most definitely."

He lowered his lips to mine and made me forget all about murder and suspects and the prospect of prison.

∾

I STRETCHED MY LEGS AND TOOK A BRACING SIP OF COFFEE before I dialed Hunter's number. As the phone rang, I wrapped the cord tightly around my right ring finger.

"Hello."

"Hunter, it's me."

"Ellison." He sounded barely awake.

"Sorry to call so early on a Sunday morning, but—"

"What's happened?"

"Nothing. Maybe. Did Anarchy tell you about the prints on my gun?"

"He did. I am going to request that all charges be dismissed. I doubt Steele will put up a fight. The man's trying to build his resumé. The last thing he wants is a high-profile loss."

I sighed. It was what we wanted, but it wasn't enough.

"Most people are happy when the charges against them are dismissed."

"I am happy. And grateful. But we both know how this town works. Unless someone else is arrested, tried, and convicted, a dark cloud will follow me for the rest of my days."

"My job is to get you off. Anarchy's job is to catch killers. Now, why did you call?"

"I told you about my conversation with Nancy Fleetwood."

"Yes."

Max leaned against my leg and looked up at me with pleading eyes. Why wasn't I taking him for a run?

"And about Trip Selden."

"Yes."

"What I didn't tell you was that I saw someone at Club K as I was leaving." I shuffled through the mail I'd failed to open yesterday—the electric bill, my Swanson's charge, my Harzfeld's charge, my Woolf's charge, my Jones Store charge, a large, heavy envelope with our names and address written in elegant calligraphy (probably a wedding invitation), and a plain envelope with my name written in a masculine scrawl.

"Who did you see?"

Ignoring the mail, I leaned back in my desk chair, tilted my head toward the ceiling, and stared. "Judge Caldwell."

"What!"

"I saw him."

"Did he see you?"

"No."

"Ellison, this is important. Say nothing to anyone. Who have you told?"

"Just Anarchy."

"Despite evidence to the contrary, Judge Caldwell is a smart man. An accusation like this could destroy his reputation, his career, his marriage, and his family. You don't want him destroyed. You want him presiding over your case."

"You just assured me the charges would be dismissed." I reached for a letter opener engraved with my former monogram and slit the top of the plain envelope.

"They will be. Probably. In the meantime, let's not antagonize the presiding judge."

Finn jumped, landing his paws on the desk.

"No!" I pushed him off.

"That's the spirit."

Oh, dear Lord. "What if Judge Caldwell did it?"

"Did what?"

"Killed Prudence."

Hunter was quiet for long seconds.

I gave the dogs a just-a-few-more-minutes look and slipped a folded sheet of paper from the envelope.

"As I remember, you visited Club K in the afternoon, shortly after lunch."

"That's right."

"Was there anyone at the club?"

"Just Mistress K—Kathleen. She said she had a private client arriving soon, so I left. I went outside and sat in my car. That's when I saw him."

"There is no way on God's green earth that Caldwell would risk his reputation by visiting a crowded sex club. I'm sure he only ever booked private sessions."

My upper lip curled with distaste. "So?"

"Prudence wouldn't have known about him. And if she didn't know, she couldn't have blackmailed him."

Hunter made perfect sense. Now. I was sure I'd find a loophole after we hung up. I opened the letter and gasped.

"What's wrong?"

"I know who Fob is. Fred Brewster."

"Prudence and Fred Brewster?" I could *hear* the curl of his upper lip. "Are you sure?"

"Fred sent me a note." I squinted, tilted my head, and tried to decipher the words. "I think he's thanking me for recounting a story about Pam. Maybe." Fred had obviously failed penmanship in school. To say that his writing resembled chicken scratch was an insult to chickens.

"So, he's a suspect."

"So is his wife."

"Ugh."

"What?"

"She has a habit of latching on at parties, like a leech. But she doesn't suck blood; she sucks any possible enjoyment from the evening. If I see her, I head the other way." Hunter so seldom said anything unkind that I was momentarily gobsmacked.

Poor Betty. Needy. Assiduously avoided. Lonely.

"Is there anything else?" he asked.

I wasn't about to tell anyone, not even my lawyer, that we'd invited friends over so that Anarchy could lift their fingerprints. "No. Nothing."

"Anarchy needs to know about Fred Brewster."

"I'll tell him as soon as we get off the phone." If he wasn't still sleeping.

"Remember, say nothing about the judge and Mistress K. I'll call you after I've talked to Steele."

We hung up, and the dogs danced, sensing their time was nigh. We went to the empty kitchen, where I clipped their leashes to their collars, and then we stepped outside.

It was still hot, but the relentless humidity had eased. The temperature was almost bearable. We ran three laps around Loose Park without incident. No squirrels, no mad dashes into backyards, no unexpected dips in the pond.

By the time we got home, I was feeling downright hopeful. This was my day. Good things were bound to happen.

Anarchy was awake and sitting at the kitchen island, nursing a cup of coffee. He wore a faded T-shirt with wrinkled pajama bottoms. His hair was mussed. And I'd never seen a more attractive man. He pulled me close and kissed the tip of my nose as the dogs flopped on the floor, their tongues lolling out of their mouths.

"I smell." My objection was half-hearted at best. I might smell awful, but I still wanted to be in his arms.

He grinned, pulling me even closer. "I don't care if you smell."

"So you admit it!"

"Would you like me to prove to you I don't care?"

"Not in the kitchen," I squeaked.

His arms drew me even closer. "Did you talk to Hunter?"

I rested my hands on his shoulders. "I did. Given the unidentified prints on the gun, he expects he can get the charges dropped."

"Wonderful news."

"It is. And Finn behaved himself at the park. It's shaping up to be a good day. Oh!"

"What?"

"I know who Fob is."

"Way to bury the lead, sweetheart." My husband sounded amused. "Who is he?"

"Fred Brewster."

"How do you know?"

"Hold on." I hurried into the family room and fetched the letter from my desk, handing it to Anarchy.

"F O B. Any idea what the O stands for?"

"None."

"What does it say?"

"I'm not entirely sure, but I think he's thanking me for telling him that his daughter rescued a child at the pool."

Aggie stepped through the back door holding two bags of groceries.

Anarchy stood immediately. "May I help you with those?" He took the heavier-looking bag from her arms and put it on the kitchen island.

"Thank you. I've been to the market to buy everything I need for a Bundt cake."

God bless Aggie. She was better than I deserved.

"You two look serious." She took a carton of eggs from the closest bag and put them on the counter. "What's up?"

"We know who Fob is."

Next, she removed a bag of chocolate chips. "Who?"

"Fred Brewster. Also, Hunter thinks he may be able to get the charges dropped."

She grinned; the expression lit her whole face. "Hurray for that! Do you still want a Bundt?"

"Yes, please," Anarchy replied. "It's not enough that the

charges are dropped. Ellison needs to be exonerated. That means we have to identify the real killer."

"Of course." Aggie lifted a bag of cake flour from the heavy-looking bag. "I'm glad I can help."

I was still stuck on Fred Brewster. Prudence had seemed so sure he would leave his wife. "Why would Fred kill Prudence?"

"Maybe she threatened his marriage or his family or his business." Anarchy shook his head in frustration. "I wish I could question him."

I reached for his hand, giving his fingers a quick squeeze. "Maybe Betty found out about the affair."

"Betty?" Aggie's eyebrows disappeared into her mop of red curls. "Betty Brewster?"

"You know her?" I asked.

"I know her housekeeper. The Brewsters pay well. Really well. If they didn't, Bernie would have quit a hundred times."

"Why?"

"Mrs. Brewster is a handful." She winced, as if remembering a particularly egregious story. "I'll call Bernie as soon as I get the cake in the oven. If Mrs. Brewster knew about her husband's philandering, Bernie will tell me."

I didn't doubt her. Not for a second. Aggie's network of housekeepers had already proved itself invaluable too many times.

CHAPTER FIFTEEN

narchy, Beau, and I stepped onto the jam-packed pool deck, and I suppressed a sigh. The word that came to mind was circus—with lots of little monkeys. Their parents crowded around the bar as the lifeguards' whistles pierced the air.

"No running, Bobby!"

"Get off the ropes, Millie."

"No food in the pool, Arthur."

Above it all, the cicadas droned, loud as lawnmowers.

I leaned toward Anarchy and whispered, "I need a drink."

"Wine?"

"Gin and tonic." The season for gin was coming to an end; I might as well indulge while I could.

"May I please get in the pool?" Beau bounced on his toes, eager to join his friends.

"Of course. Have fun and be safe."

He was gone before I finished speaking.

Anarchy and I walked to the bar together, joining the back of the line.

"Good turnout," he observed. "Especially for a Sunday night."

"The last night of summer. Tomorrow night, every parent here will be fighting with their kids about bedtimes."

"Even us?"

"Probably not." Beau caused no waves, which sometimes worried me (when I wasn't worried about going to prison). It was almost as if he feared we might send him away if he caused us problems. Nothing could be further from the truth. We were his family now; nothing would ever change that.

"Good evening, Mrs. Jones."

I turned and smiled at Courtland. "Good evening. The pool deck looks marvelous."

He winced. "You should know, there are vegetables on the kids' buffet."

"How did she manage that?" Anne Everist was nothing if not determined.

"She called the club manager."

"How tiresome for you." And shame on the manager for not having Courtland's back.

"I just wanted you to know."

My answering smile was wry. "I've got bigger things to worry about than vegetables."

He stepped closer to us and lowered his voice. "Was the list helpful?"

"Very," Anarchy replied.

To my knowledge, it hadn't been, but Courtland had risked angering every person listed by giving us those names. "We are very grateful."

"My pleasure. Enjoy your evening." He turned away, off to solve a problem.

"Courtland?"

He looked over his shoulder.

"Is Sissy MacIntyre on the reservation list?"

It was his turn for a wry smile. "She is not."

"Good," Anarchy growled. With his hands in the pockets of his khaki pants and a slightly bored expression on his handsome face, Anarchy looked like half the insouciant men on the pool deck, but I didn't need to hear him growl to recognize an under-current of anger in him. Sissy's attack on me was neither forgiven nor forgotten.

I stepped forward as the line moved. "That's a relief." People whispered enough without Sissy around to encourage them. "Thank you, Courtland."

He nodded and melted into the crowd.

A moment later, we had our drinks, a beer and a G&T with two limes, both in red plastic cups.

"Cheers." Anarchy tapped the white rim of his cup against mine. "Ready?"

Nope, but I didn't have a choice. It was time to face the crowd of chattering club members, some of whom thought I was a killer (though everyone agreed that Prudence had it coming).

"You've got this." Anarchy rested his hand on the small of my back, and I gave him a quick smile.

We stepped into the fray.

Liz caught me first. "Great dress."

"This old thing?" I wore one of last year's Lilly shifts in the zoo print. "Thank you. You look marvelous, too."

She smoothed her khaki linen shift. "We had the best time last night, thanks for including us."

"Our pleasure. We'll have to do it again soon."

"Perry wants me to get Aggie's recipe for cheese puffs. Do you think she'd part with it?"

"I'll ask her." Aggie's Bundt cake recipe was a closely guarded secret, but she might share her cheese puffs.

"Thank you. Perry *loved* them. He ate far more than his fair share." She frowned at someone over my shoulder. "Is that Betty Brewster?"

"Betty?" I frowned. "The Brewsters aren't members."

Liz glanced down at her Bernardos. "Perry's on the pool committee; he told me we're honoring Pam tonight. Did you hear? She saved a little girl from drowning. I don't understand how Pam can be so lovely when she grew up with a mother like Betty. At any rate, I wonder if her parents are here for the presentation."

Her eyes widened, giving her a slightly panicked look. "Ellison, Anarchy, sorry to do this, but will you please excuse me?" She disappeared before I could answer.

"Ellison, it's so nice to see you again! Is this your husband?" Betty's voice was shrill…and eager.

I tried not to gape at her, hard to do when she'd worn a revealing silk cocktail dress, stilettos, and a king's ransom in diamonds to a pool party. The dress, a bordello red, hugged her in all the wrong places. And the updo? There would be copious bugs caught in her hairspray before the evening's end.

"He's so handsome," Betty stage-whispered.

"I think so."

"Ellison gave Pam her first babysitting job. We've always been so fond of her." It wasn't clear if she meant me or Grace.

I didn't ask for clarification. "Pam was a wonderful babysitter."

"Is Grace here?" Betty swiveled her head as if she'd be able to pick Grace out of the crowd.

"I'm not sure. She's coming with friends."

Betty's brow furrowed. "It's so hard when they decide they don't need us anymore."

I blinked. How had we gone from Grace arriving separately to her not needing me? "Anarchy, I don't believe you've met Betty Brewster."

"I haven't had the pleasure." He gave her his most charming smile, and she swayed on her heels and fanned her face, blinking rapidly.

"My goodness, you're handsome. I wish I could introduce you to Fred. He's around her somewhere." She pouted. "He abandoned me the minute we arrived. But that's men for you. They'd rather talk the stock market, drink whiskey, and smoke cigars than spend time with their wives."

Since my husband was by my side, I didn't comment.

"His loss is our gain."

I side-eyed Anarchy, who was laying it on a bit thick. But Betty didn't seem to notice. Instead, she giggled like a teenage girl. "Handsome and charming. You got a good one, Ellison. Hold on tight." Her gaze scanned the crowd, a slightly manic look in her pale blue eyes. "I bet half the women here would love to steal him. My advice is to keep a weather eye." She jabbed me with her elbow. "Constant vigilance."

Oh, dear Lord. No wonder Fred had strayed. The woman was a complete mess.

We had to be wrong about her. No one this oblivious could successfully plan and execute a murder. Unless it was an act. She'd have to be an Oscar-caliber actress to make this level of crazy believable. And I believed. I looked into her desperate eyes, and I believed.

"Mom, what are you doing here?" Pam looked pale beneath her tan.

"I can't tell you; it would ruin the surprise." Betty's smile was wide and satisfied.

"This is a party for club members." Pam kept her voice low as her gaze scanned the crowd. Her hands clenched. Her face flushed. And her lips thinned. She looked like she wanted the ground to open up and swallow her whole.

"We're guests."

Pam narrowed her eyes, and she glared at me as if I were responsible for her mother's presence. "Dad's here too?"

"Somewhere. You know how your father is. He can never be bothered to keep me company. And it's not as if I know many of the members here. That's why I was so pleased to see Ellison and her husband. You remember Ellison. And have you met her husband? Anarchy, this is my daughter.

"Pleased to meet you."

Pam's face was a mask of pure mortification. "Who invited you, Mom? Please tell me you didn't crash this party."

"Of course not! I attended one party—one—without an invitation, and you and your father will never let me forget it."

"It was the Jewel Ball, Mom."

Wow. Crashing a debutante ball took a level of nerve I didn't possess. It had never, not once, occurred to me that anyone might crash that ball. The embarrassment of being escorted out? Something within me withered at the mere thought.

"I asked for an invitation. I was perfectly willing to buy a ticket, and they wouldn't sell me one."

"Because it's exclusive." Pam raked her fingers through her hair. "Mom, who invited you tonight?"

I spoke up, trying to calm her agitation. "The pool committee may have extended an invitation."

Pam frowned at me. "Why?"

"They're recognizing you this evening."

"Ellison, you ruined the surprise!"

Pam ignored her mom's outburst. "And they invited my mother?"

"Don't be mean, Pammie." Betty's voice wobbled. "You know I just want to be with you."

"Please don't call me that." Pam pinched the bridge of her nose. "What are you wearing, Mom?"

I'd thought the same thing, but sympathy flared in my chest when I saw the flash of pain in Betty's eyes.

"It's a party at the country club."

"A pool party, Mom." Pam waved at my Lilly shift and low-heeled espadrilles. "It's casual. We should get Dad to take you home."

"Good luck with that. Your father disappeared."

"Disappeared where?"

"Who knows? Maybe he's on the golf course with some strumpet." Betty's casual malice hung in the air.

"Mom!"

"What?"

"Mr. and Mrs. Jones, please excuse us." Pam grabbed her mother's arm and dragged her away, pulling her through the crowd as if she were a misbehaving child.

"The next time I complain about Mother, remind me of that conversation."

Anarchy flashed me a grin. "Betty seemed very concerned about strumpets on the golf course."

"Do you think that woman is actually capable of murder?"

"Never underestimate crazy."

"Poor Pam." Poor Fred.

We mingled. We had a second round of drinks. Night was falling when we went through the buffet. Thanks to a bit of maneuvering on my part, we found ourselves at the same dinner table as Lucia and Trip Selden.

"Lucia, Trip, do you know Anarchy?"

"Pleasure." Trip extended his hand.

"Likewise."

I put my plate and rolled silverware on the table and took the seat next to Lucia's. "I understand you're back from Greece."

"It was fabulous. It's a trip everyone should take. So much history, beautiful beaches, and the shopping wasn't half bad." She swung her feet out from under the table so I could admire her sandals.

"Anarchy, we're going to Greece next summer."

He gave me an indulgent smile.

"Do you get much time off?" asked Trip.

Anarchy ignored Trip's condescending tone. "I'm fortunate that I can take unpaid leave if the occasion calls for it."

"The joys of marrying a rich woman."

"Trip!" Lucia sounded only mildly outraged.

I was fully outraged. "Anarchy doesn't need my money."

"Of course he doesn't." The condescension positively dripped. No wonder Trip and Henry had been such good friends. They were both complete jerks.

I hoped Trip had killed Prudence. Mainly because I wanted him to rot in prison.

"My husband graduated from Stanford. He is the smartest man I've ever met. If he decided to go into business, he'd be hugely successful."

"Yet, he's a cop."

My blood boiled, and I ignored Anarchy's restraining touch on my arm. "Anarchy is a cop because it's his way of giving back. He doesn't need to work. He does it because he wants to make the world a better place."

"Nice to have a woman fight your battles."

I stood and picked up my plate and silverware. "I think we need to find another table."

"Ellison—" Lucia shot her husband a death glare before reaching for my arm "—he didn't mean it. He was joking."

That was precisely what people said when someone reacted to their bad behavior. *I was only joking. Can't you take a joke?*

"He meant it." I narrowed my eyes and bit my tongue. Anarchy didn't want people to know about his family's holdings, and I wouldn't broadcast them now. However, Trip's firm represented one of the Jones family's businesses based in the Midwest, and if I had anything to say about it, that would change on Tuesday. "Trip, Prudence mentioned you the last time I talked to her. She said you two were regulars at some club. Did you join another one?" Prudence had mentioned no such thing. Saying she had was catty and small and beneath me, and I didn't care. I was too busy enjoying the way Trip turned green beneath his tan. "Come on, Anarchy, let's go sit with the Hubbells."

With an apologetic nod at Lucia, Anarchy stood.

We'd only walked a few feet when he stopped me. "Remind me never to make you mad."

"Ha. Just don't insult my husband."

"Do you really want to eat with the Hubbells?"

"No. Let's go sit on the patio wall." We'd have to walk around the side of the clubhouse and climb a hill, but the privacy and the quiet would make it worthwhile. We could stare at the stars in the night sky, eat in peace, and discuss suspects without fear of being overheard.

We'd rounded the corner, and the noise from the party had begun to fade when my foot caught. I tripped, and my plate went flying as I fell onto my hands and knees, eye level with Betty Brewster's unseeing gaze.

CHAPTER SIXTEEN

"You just fell over a body." Anarchy's voice was almost disbelieving.

"It's dark. I didn't see her." I sounded defensive.

"Ellison, you just fell over a body."

"Don't pretend to be surprised." It was hardly the first time I'd happened upon a body (although I couldn't remember the last time I'd tripped over one). Still on the ground, I inched away from Betty's corpse, the grass digging into the heels of my hands. "What killed her?"

Out of nowhere, Anarchy produced a tiny flashlight. "There's a dark patch under her head."

"Someone fractured her skull."

"You sound like a medical examiner."

This wasn't my first rodeo. "If you'll stay with her, I'll find Courtland."

"We need to call the station."

"We need to give these parents a chance to get their kids home before they realize there's been a murder."

"Everyone here is a suspect."

I could see it, every single club member at the party forced to sit around the pool as the police interviewed them. One by one. A long, arduous endeavor. Tired, scared, and whining to go home. And that was the adults; the children would be even worse. "Courtland has their names and phone numbers. Do we really want to traumatize a hundred children?" I hit his soft spot.

"Fine," he ceded. "Find Courtland."

I stood, brushing off my hands and knees before I lifted onto my tiptoes and kissed his cheek. "Thank you for understanding. I'll be back as soon as I can."

"Be careful."

Somehow, I didn't think the killer was interested in me.

I skirted the edge of the party until I found a busboy. "I need to speak to Courtland Gerhardt."

The young man rested his tray on the edge of a freshly cleared table. "I'm not sure where he is."

"Then find him. It's an emergency."

"Yes, ma'am." He picked up his tray and headed toward the clubhouse.

I rolled my eyes. Courtland actively managed parties. He wasn't in the clubhouse. He was outside with the members, keeping a watchful eye on the pool, the bar, and the two buffets.

I headed toward the buffets now (taking no small satisfaction in noting the vegetables on the kids' table were untouched). Courtland wasn't there. My next stop was the bar, where I cut the line and asked the bartender, "Have you seen Courtland?"

"Lifeguard tower."

I hurried to the pool and found Courtland watching the monkeys play in the water. "I need to talk to you. It's important."

"Sure." He frowned as we stepped back from the water. "What's wrong?"

I leaned close and whispered, "I found a body."

He grinned at me, anticipating a punchline.

There wasn't one. I shook my head.

"I'm sorry." He pressed his fingers to his forehead as he realized I wasn't joking. "You did what?"

"I found a body."

"I feel like we just did this."

"I didn't find Prudence." The distinction was important.

His shoulders slumped. "Where?"

"The snack-bar side of the clubhouse. Anarchy and I were walking up to the patio when I tripped over—when I found her. It looks like murder."

"Who is it?"

"Betty Brewster." And I had a terrible feeling I knew who'd killed her.

"At least it's not a member." Later, when he wasn't reeling, Courtland would regret that remark. But in the moment, and faced with a second murder in a week, I understood where he was coming from. "What do we do?"

"End the party."

His gaze took in the pool filled with children, the adults sipping cocktails, the diners who lingered at their tables. "How?"

"Lie. Tell everyone there's a concern about a gas leak. They'll grab their kids and be gone in a New York minute."

"It's as if you've done this before."

I leveled a look at him. "Don't quit your day job for comedy."

He grinned at me before heading to the lifeguard desk. A moment later, his voice came on the loudspeaker. "Ladies and gentlemen, someone has smelled gas. Out of an abundance of caution, we ask you to collect your children and head home."

An angry buzz followed.

"Again, for your children's safety, we ask that you head home."

A phalanx of thin-lipped mothers marched toward the pool, demanding that their children get out of the water *right this minute*.

Within a few minutes, the pool deck was almost empty.

A wet hand tugged on my fingers. "Ellison?" Beau sounded scared.

I crouched, wrapped my arms around his wet body, and dropped a kiss on his head. "Everything will be okay."

"Do we need to leave?"

"We'll go in a little while. There's something Anarchy has to do first."

"Mom?"

"Grace, you're still here. Would you please take Beau home?"

"It's the telethon. At Kimberly's." Their tradition. I had a bad habit of upending her life; I wouldn't take this from her.

"Right. Can you stay with Beau while I talk to Anarchy? I'll be back in five minutes."

Her eyes narrowed. "There's no gas leak."

"No."

"You found a body." An accusation, not a question.

I shrugged. "Five minutes, Grace."

"Fine."

"Beau, you stay with Grace, okay?"

He looked at me with huge eyes and nodded.

I trudged back to Anarchy and found Courtland already there. "The pool deck is basically empty. I need to take Beau home."

"And I need to call this in."

"I can stay with the body while you make the call, Mr. Jones. Should I get a tablecloth and cover her?"

"No!" Anarchy and I spoke as one.

"Don't touch her," Anarchy continued. "Don't touch anything. We don't want to disturb any evidence." He raked his fingers through his hair. "Where's the nearest phone?"

"Lifeguard desk," Courtland replied.

"Come on." I tugged on his hand. "I'll show you."

Together, we walked back to the empty pool, and I pointed to the desk. "Dial nine for an outside line. I love you, and I'll see you when you get home."

Grace and Beau huddled on a nearby chaise.

"Where's Kimberly?"

"She left. I'll drive to her house when we're done."

"We're done. Thanks for staying." I smiled and held out my hand to Beau. "Are you ready to go home?"

He paused, not taking my hand. "You found a body?"

"I'm afraid so."

"You don't seem sad."

"No."

"Or scared."

"I hide it well." I crouched until we were at eye level. "Do you remember your first time on a skateboard?"

He nodded.

"Were you scared?"

"I guess."

"How about the second time? Or the tenth? You're a smart kid; you know that whenever you ride, you might fall off and get hurt. That's scary." At least it was scary to me. Watching Beau fly down the street on a board with four wheels and no brakes gave me heart palpitations. "The first time I found a body—" I couldn't help but glance at the pool "—I was terrified. It's still scary when I find one, but I've gotten better at handling the fear."

"Why do you do it?"

"Believe me, honey, it's not on purpose."

"She's unlucky," Grace spoke with a degree of ennui unique to teenage girls. "But she's also really strong. And she'll always take care of us."

Beau took my hand as I mouthed a silent "thank you" to my daughter.

Still clutching Beau's small hand, I stood. "Grace, we'll walk you to your car."

We waved at Anarchy, who was still deep in conversation, and headed up the hill to the parking lot. We were halfway to the top when a thought hit me hard enough to make me stumble.

"Mom?"

"We need to go back."

"What? No. You said you were going home."

"Five minutes, Grace. I have to talk to Anarchy." Taking in her mulish expression, I added, "Someone may be in danger."

"Fine." She drew out the long "I," letting me know with one syllable what an imposition it was.

We hurried back to the pool deck, and I breathed a relieved sigh when I saw my husband still on the phone.

His eyes widened as I walked toward him. "Hold on." He covered the receiver's mouthpiece with his hand. "What's wrong?"

"Where's Fred Brewster?"

He scanned the empty pool deck.

"Either he killed her or he's in trouble."

Anarchy nodded slowly. "You don't think he killed her."

It stretched the limits of credulity to think there might be two murderers at the same country club at the same time. And, as far as I could tell, Fred had no reason to kill Prudence. "No."

Anarchy uncovered the mouthpiece. "Peters, bring extra uniforms. We need to search the clubhouse and golf course."

"I'll see you at home."

"I'll be late."

I gave him a tired smile. "I know."

I reclaimed Beau's hand, and we saw Grace to her car, waiting until she was safely buckled with the ignition running. Only then did we walk to Anarchy's vehicle.

"Grace is right."

"About?" I unlocked the doors.

"You're brave."

We climbed into the car, and I slid the key into the ignition. "Bravery is just putting one foot in front of the other."

"It's more than that."

"Is it?"

He nodded, his expression solemn. "You take risks for others." His gaze dropped to his lap. "Like me."

"Honey, you were no risk. Welcoming you into our family was a blessing."

He crossed his arms. "You know what I mean."

"I do."

"Just remember, when you're taking risks, that there are people who need you."

My heart clenched. "I'll remember. I promise."

"Who died?"

"A lady named Betty Brewster, her daughter was a lifeguard at the club."

"Which one?"

"Pam."

Beau wrinkled his nose.

"You don't like her?"

"I guess she's okay." Hardly a ringing endorsement.

"Just okay?"

"She yelled at Bobby for running on the pool deck."

"That was her job." And Bobby didn't listen to polite requests.

"Like, really yelled. She seemed crazy."

I tightened my hands around the steering wheel.

We arrived home and piled out of the car, heading for the back door. The door that didn't require my key. My lips thinned. I'd talked to both the kids about the importance of locking the doors, and Grace, who'd left for the club after we did, had already forgotten.

The dogs greeted us with wagging tails and eager grins before racing into the darkest corners of the backyard.

Beau yawned, a long, drawn-out yawn that showcased his tonsils.

"Cover your mouth, honey."

"Sorry," he mumbled.

"You should get ready for bed."

"I'm not sleepy." He yawned again.

"I'll tell you what, go get ready for bed, and then we can curl up on the couch and watch the telethon." Maybe I'd get lucky and see Frank Sinatra.

"Okay." He trudged up the stairs, his steps heavy on the treads.

I poured myself a glass of water and headed into the family room. I too was tired, but there was no way I could sleep. Not with the night's events so fresh in my mind. Not with the suspicions bouncing around my brain like a demented pinball.

My fingers were on the light switch when a flat voice said, "You're home earlier than I expected."

My heart leaped to my throat, and every muscle in my body went rigid. Barely keeping hold of the glass in my left hand, I used my right hand to flip the switch, flooding the room with light. "Hello, Pam."

"You don't seem surprised to see me." Her expression was mildly surprised, as if she'd expected me to scream or cry.

Sadly, she wasn't the first killer to sneak into my house. My days of screaming and crying were well behind me.

I wasn't even particularly worried, not until I looked into her eyes. They were cold as January. That's when fear iced my spine. Beau would be entering this room in a minute or two, and I refused to put him at risk. "How did you get in?"

"The last time I was here, I swiped an extra set of keys from the junk drawer."

"Do you mind if I sit?" I nodded toward my desk.

From her spot in the club chair nearest the fireplace, she nodded. Her hands were loose in her lap, but I had to wonder if she had a weapon. Perhaps a gun hidden in the pocket of her dress. I searched for a suspicious bulge.

I sat and gently, quietly, discreetly cracked the desk's center drawer. "Why are you here?"

"To apologize." A small, humorless smile curled her lips. "I didn't mean for you to be accused."

There! My questing fingers had found the hidden key. I slid it out of the drawer. "You killed Prudence."

"I heard what she said at the pool, that my dad was going to divorce my mom for her." She spoke in a monotone. "I couldn't let that happen."

"Why not?"

"My mom is too much for one person to handle. If Dad left her, that one person would be me. You heard her." She gave a sharp, bitter laugh. "You saw her. She's needy and oblivious and selfish."

"But murder?"

"I didn't have a choice." She was calm, almost clinical, in her defense.

"How?"

"The head lifeguard let me go home after I saved Suzie. I came here, instead. I knew where you kept your gun from when I babysat Grace." She shook her head. "I wasn't expecting the second dog, but he accepted me after Max gave me a lick."

Max and I would have words about warm welcomes for murderous thieves.

"How did you get Prudence to the golf course?" My voice shook.

"That was easy." She sat a little straighter, as if she were proud of how clever she'd been. "I took a sheet of paper from my dad's monogrammed pad and asked her to meet me on the golf course at eleven. Dad and I both have terrible handwriting. I knew she wouldn't be able to tell that I'd written the note, not him. When she showed up, I shot her." A shadow passed over her features, a flash of emotion I couldn't identify. Regret?

"It's easy to think about murder, harder to pull the trigger."

"Oh no, I had no problem pulling the trigger." Her gaze, a terrifying void, met mine. "She was a terrible woman. No, the hardest part was the panic afterwards. I didn't expect the sweating or the trembling or the way my heart tried to beat its way out of my chest. Had someone heard the shot? Were they coming? I got so flustered that I dropped the gun, and I couldn't find it in the grass. I crawled around in the dark, knowing that every second I spent looking for it meant that someone might arrive to investigate the noise. So, I gave up."

Leaving my gun behind.

She glanced down at her hands in her lap. "You know what's funny?"

So far, nothing. I slipped the key into the right-hand drawer. "What?"

"I think she was lying. Dad didn't seem sad that she was dead. If he'd cared about her, he would have mourned. I don't think he was going to leave Mom." She'd killed a woman in error, and her voice was uncaring, flat as a pancake.

"What about your mother?"

"She figured it out. Apparently, she checked my room the night I killed Prudence. Do you know what she told me tonight?"

I shook my head and eased the drawer open.

"She thought I did it for her. To save her marriage. She said that she was glad that I'd killed Prudence because now I'd have to stay with her forever." For the first time since I'd entered the room, Pam's face showed actual emotion—pure, unadulterated loathing. "I killed Prudence to get away from that woman. And instead, I gave her the leverage she needed to hold onto me forever."

From the kitchen, I could hear the dogs barking at the back door.

Pam stood. "Like I said, I wanted to apologize. It can't be easy, being accused of murder."

"Your mother? How?" I slid my hand into the drawer.

"Easy. I told her Dad was on the patio with another woman. If she wanted to catch them in the act, she needed to sneak around the side of the clubhouse. When she stepped into the shadows, I hit her over the head with a hammer I swiped from the maintenance room."

I searched Pam's face for a shred of remorse and found none. Then I searched the drawer and found it empty. A pit opened in my stomach as my fingers scrabbled at nothing.

"Looking for this?" Pam smiled and pointed my gun at me. "You really need to find better hiding places for your weapons."

"So it seems."

The dogs careened into the family room, dancing on their paws and jumping over each other in their eagerness to join us.

"I'm leaving now." She edged toward the door.

I wasn't about to stop her. Better she escape than put Beau at risk. Also, I'd promised him, not thirty minutes ago, that I would be there for him. Stopping Pam wasn't worth a bullet. "What will you do?"

"Start over somewhere far from here."

"I don't think so." Anarchy stood in the doorway with his gun aimed at Pam's chest.

"Can you shoot me before I shoot your wife?" Her smug smile said she knew the answer.

"Yes." Anarchy fired, hitting her arm.

Pam gasped, and the weapon fell to the floor.

He stepped forward, kicking the fallen weapon away from her.

When the ringing in my ears faded, I asked, "How did you know to come home?"

"Beau heard voices. He called the club and wouldn't hang up until someone fetched me."

"Where is he?" I was overwhelmed with the need to hug our little boy.

"I'm here." Beau barreled into the room and launched himself into my arms, nearly knocking the breath out of me.

I didn't care. I hugged him as tightly as I could. "Thank you, Beau. You're a hero. How can I ever thank you?"

"Promise not to find any more bodies."

I brushed a lock of hair off his forehead and gave a regretful smile. "Sweetie, I don't make promises I can't keep."

CHAPTER SEVENTEEN

Anarchy, Hunter, Aggie, and I gathered at the kitchen island, sipping morning coffee.

"Thank you for coming over." I smiled at my lawyer.

He tilted his coffee mug in acknowledgment. "My pleasure. Please, tell me exactly what happened last night. I already have the gist, but I want the unvarnished details."

We recounted finding Betty's body and the details of Pam's family room confession.

"What happened to Fred?" Hunter asked.

"Fred and Pam left the party together," Anarchy replied. He'd spent much of the night interrogating Pam and had all the answers. "She told him she wanted to skip the ceremony because she knew Betty would embarrass her. When they got home, she planted the hammer she used to kill Betty in his sock drawer."

I looked up from my coffee mug. "Why would she do that? She confessed."

Anarchy reached for my hand, and his thumb stroked across my knuckles. "I don't think she planned on letting you live to repeat what she'd told you."

I frowned my confusion. "Why? Why come here at all?"

Anarchy shook his head and gave a tired sigh. "There's something profoundly wrong with that young woman. I suspect she wanted at least one person to know what she'd done."

Coffee roiled in my stomach. I'd been way too sanguine, sure that Pam wouldn't hurt me unless I pushed her. I'd put Beau at risk.

He leaned forward and brushed a kiss across my cheek. "We're all safe now."

"What about the people Prudence blackmailed?" Aggie's voice was aggressively bright, as if her sunshine could erase Pam's darkness. "What happens to them?"

"They didn't break any laws," Anarchy replied. "They have nothing to worry about. And maybe they've learned an important lesson about discretion."

I gave my husband a sharp look. We both knew that wasn't true. I'd come across Hubb and Malcolm kissing in Malcolm's backyard. Hardly discreet, not when a neighbor might look out a window or a wayward dog might lead his owner straight to them. "It's a shame you can't find a charge for Trip."

Hunter swirled the coffee in his mug before smiling at me over the rim. "Speaking of charges. I called Steele at home. Assuming Pam's prints are on your gun, it's over. No arraignment. No charges. You're done."

"I bet he's disappointed." I couldn't keep the bitterness out of my voice.

"No," said Anarchy. "Morrison is the disappointed one. His little vendetta against me failed. You should be getting a written apology in the next day or two."

An apology? "Is that usual?"

"No. But the rush to arrest you for murder wasn't usual either. Peters tells me that Morrison is putting in for retirement."

I couldn't keep that catty smile off my lips. My time in jail still rankled. The thought of jail made me think of my cellmate. "Hunter, how much do I owe you for representing Darla?"

"The firm will send the bill."

"How did you get the charges against her dropped?"

"I just pointed out to the man who'd filed them that a trial wasn't in his best interests. I promised to drag him and his company through the mud. I said I'd subpoena every woman who'd ever left his employ. The case would be long and expensive and grueling. He decided that he had more to lose than Darla did."

"Thank you. She's coming in for an interview tomorrow."

"Wait." Anarchy frowned at me. "You're hiring your cellmate? Where?"

"The bank."

"Because jail is where financial institutions should find their employees."

I swatted at his arm. "Sarcasm does not become you, detective. Besides, I have a feeling about her. A good feeling."

The oven dinged, and Aggie slid out two sheets of chocolate chip cookies before hitting us all with a narrow-eyed glare. "Give them a minute to cool."

The back door burst open, and Libba rushed in, her face radiant. "I did it!"

"Did what?"

"I said 'yes.'" She held out her left hand so that I could admire the enormous diamond weighing down her ring finger.

"You told him your big secret, and it didn't matter." I knew Charlie wouldn't care about her past.

She flushed. "Not exactly. I decided to take Cricket and Mimi's advice. Some secrets are meant to be kept." She waved her ring under my nose. "You'll be my matron of honor."

"I'd be honored. When's the wedding?"

"Soon. Why wait? Just promise me something."

"Anything."

"No bodies the week of my wedding."

Why did people keep asking me to make promises beyond my control? "I'll do my best."

Turn the page for my new series!

MEET FREDDIE ARCHER

Inspired by one of the first real-life columnists at The New Yorker, Freddie writes a column about the glamorous world of New York in the 1920s.

Bony Johnson is the son of a woman who helped raise Freddie. He's twelve-years old, owner of the sweetest smile in Manhattan, and in real danger. Bony has been running numbers for Red Garrett. Not necessarily dangerous, except a thug has been robbing Red's boys.

When a child is murdered, it's up to Freddie to keep Bony safe and catch a killer, all while making sure she doesn't miss the deadline for her next column.

If you enjoy the Lady Eleanor Swift mysteries, the Penelope Banks murder mysteries, or the Royal Spyness mysteries, you'll probably like Freddie.

Thanks so much for giving her a try!

Julie Mulhern is the USA TODAY bestselling author of The Country Club Murders. She stumbled across a column by Lois Long and wished they could be friends. Time machines being hard to come by, Julie did the next best thing, and used Lois as inspiration for Freddie Archer.

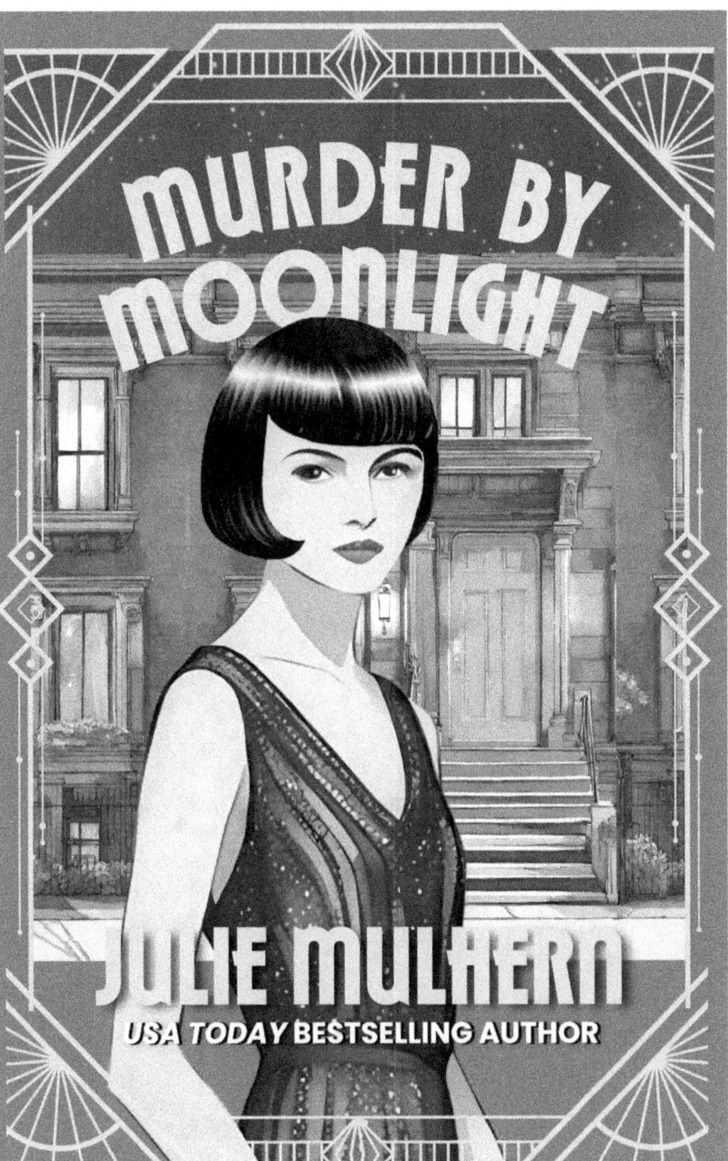

MURDER BY MOONLIGHT
JULIE MULHERN
USA TODAY BESTSELLING AUTHOR

MURDER BY MOONLIGHT

CHAPTER 1

Taken from A Touch of Rouge
April 4, 1925, issue of *Gotham Magazine*

Last night, I found myself at a table for two at the packed Lido Club. To my left, a couple so green behind the ears, one could practically smell daffodils and fresh grass. To my right, a couple so dripping with ennui that a puddle formed around their ankles.

The young man took direction—what to order, when to dance, and had a ready light for his date's cigarette.

The older man ordered for two, refused to dance, and let his wife light her own cigarette. She said not a word in protest.

Boys will be boys and men will be men? Perhaps the ladies should demand more.

At any rate, the Lido was filled with smartly dressed people. And really, the older couple didn't miss much by keeping to their table. The dance floor was too crowded to move. Such are the joys of spring.

. . .

Nick smirked at Freddie. Smirked. As if knowing about a new club before she did was a feather in his cap. As if he'd won a contest.

Perhaps, in his mind, he had. Her job at *Gotham* included writing about clubs and speakeasies and restaurants. As such, she stayed current on the latest openings.

This place, The Red Door, she'd missed.

Freddie suspected she hadn't missed much.

There were scads of walk-up speakeasies on the Upper East Side and in Midtown. And the Village? Every other door was a speak. They didn't need to motor all the way to Harlem to find one. She paused on the cracked sidewalk, taking in the spiffy red door, made smarter by the condition of its neighbors, a laundry with dingy windows a sepia-toned cigar store.

The other people on the sidewalk—people in evening clothes who were presumably eager to reach their destinations—grumbled at the woman who lingered, impeding the flow of traffic.

Her gaze still fixed on the red door, Freddie asked, "Why this place?"

"There's a singer I'd like to hear." Nick produced shows on Broadway. He was always on the lookout for new talent.

"Miss Freddie?"

She turned.

The yellow glow cast by the nearest streetlight revealed a boy made up of knobby knees, sharp elbows, and big, dark eyes.

"Bony!" she exclaimed in delight.

Bony smiled. That smile. The sweetest, friendliest expression to ever grace a face. It melted her heart every time she saw it.

"What a fantabulous surprise. Give me a hug." She wrapped her arms around the boy, squeezing his narrow shoulders.

Nick coughed.

Bony squirmed.

Reluctantly, she allowed him his freedom. Then she glanced at her watch and frowned. Surely a child Bony's age should be in bed. What was he doing on the streets at this hour?

As if he'd read her mind, he held up a policy book. "Place a bet?"

"Bony Johnson, what in tarnation are you doing?" She sounded like her mother—ugh—but the situation called for a censorious tone.

His smile faltered, and he ducked his head.

Nick, who waited next to her, gave his wristwatch an exaggerated glance. "Freddie, they're holding a table."

She ignored him. The club would hold his table until Christmas, and they both knew it. "Where's your mother?" she asked Bony. Did Penelope know her son was in the numbers game?

Bony's smile disappeared entirely. "She's not doing so good."

Penelope Johnson, her parents' upstairs maid for nearly twenty years, had helped raise her. When Penelope left their employ for a better job, Freddie had wept. She'd missed Penelope and Bony terribly. "What's wrong?"

Bony's shoulders hunched, and he studied the sidewalk. "Cancer."

Freddie's heart sank. Was Penelope so ill that Bony had to keep a policy book to support her? "I'm so sorry. May I visit her?" She'd take fresh flowers and a hamper of food. She'd offer money, and Penelope would refuse. Freddie would insist. And prevail. Not because she was particularly persuasive. No, she'd prevail because Penelope adored her son and wanted the best for him. The best did not include taking nickel bets on street corners at a time when children should be in bed.

"She's not taking visitors, but I'll tell her you asked after her."

"Hear that?" Nick gave her elbow a tug. "He'll give her your regards. Let's go, doll."

Freddie swallowed a frustrated sigh. If she talked to Penelope, she'd find a way to get Bony off the streets. Her eyes narrowed on the book clutched in Bony's left hand. "How much do you need before you can go home?"

"Two dollars."

"Then that's what I'll bet." She handed over two bills.

The boy accepted the money, and his smile made a return. "Your numbers?"

"Six-two-seven."

His gaze caught hers. He knew what those numbers meant. He gave a quick nod, made a note in his book, and presented her with a receipt. "Thank you, Miss Freddie."

"Bony, I want you to come see me at the magazine office. *Gotham*. You know the address?"

He nodded.

"This week." She speared him with a serious gaze. "I mean it."

"Yes, Miss Freddie." He shuffled his feet as if he were eager to be gone, and she doubted his sincerity.

"I'll see you soon, Bony." If she didn't, she'd track him down. Surely a member of her parents' staff kept in touch with his mother.

Bony nodded—too quickly.

Next to her, Nick bristled, a veritable porcupine of impatience, but he still held out his hand to Bony. "Nick Peters."

They shook. When they separated, Bony glanced at his palm, and his eyes widened.

"Keep it," said Nick. "Get yourself a good dinner."

"Thank you, sir." Bony slipped his hand into his pocket. "Nice seeing you, Miss Freddie."

"Likewise. I'll see you again soon."

Bony trotted away.

"What did you give him?" she asked Nick.

"Ten dollars. The boy looks like he needs to eat more."

Ten dollars would buy Bony two weeks' worth of dinners. Nick's easy generosity was one of his best qualities.

"How do you know him?"

"His mother used to work for my parents. When he was little, she brought him to work."

"How old is he?"

"Thirteen. Or is it fourteen?"

"He should be home. In bed."

She didn't disagree. "You heard him. His mother is sick."

"Be that as it may, you shouldn't encourage his current line of work."

Nick regularly bet royal sums in casinos, and he was scolding her for a two-dollar bet? Or maybe he disapproved of Bony taking bets? If the boy needed to support his mother, running numbers was a better way to make a living than toiling in a sweat shop.

She tamped down her excellent points. Nick didn't necessarily appreciate it when she made sense. He was too sure of his own opinions. She'd long since discovered it was easier to hold her tongue than listen to his detailed explanation of all the ways she was mistaken.

Clearly mistaking her silence for agreement, he gently guided her toward the red door. "How do you select your numbers?"

"I always bet those numbers." June twenty-seventh. Grey's birthday. He'd have turned thirty this summer, if he'd returned home from the war. "In memory of my brother."

A frown darkened Nick's handsome face. Truly, the man was ridiculously handsome, with strong cheek bones, full lips, a divot in his chin, and dark blond hair. When he smiled, he was devastating. When he frowned, he looked like a spoiled child. "How often do you bet?"

"Why on earth do you care?" She had plenty of money—the

trust her grandparents had left her, and her job at *Gotham*—a few bets didn't begin to make a dint.

"It's unseemly. And you might lose." Was he worried about appearances or her?

"You play roulette and poker." And he regularly lost.

"That's different."

"Why?"

"It's in a casino, not on the street." Nick bet in a posh environment where men in tuxedos and ladies in silk evening gowns sipped Champagne or good scotch before they rolled the dice. When Nick handed over his money, he received chips, not a slightly grubby paper receipt like the one she'd slipped into her evening bag.

Gambling was gambling.

Nick's bets at a casino lined its owner's pockets. The numbers games fueled Harlem. Bony's boss and men like him loaned money to black businessmen (the ones white bankers wouldn't let through their doors). They invested in community schools and programs. They gave money to worthy causes.

Nick opened the door, and his hand on her lower back propelled her inside.

The club was dark, its rough edges softened by a haze of blue smoke. In the corner, a trio played passable jazz. A bar made from a heavy, ebony-stained wood stretched across the back wall. Behind it, a mirror reached for the tin ceiling. As speaks went, she'd seen it a thousand times. She'd smelled it a thousand times too—stale cocktails, smoke, sweat, cloying perfume, and pomade.

Nick led her to a small table near the players and pulled out her chair.

She sat, and Nick joined her, reaching for her hand. "Thank you for coming with me. You should write about this place."

Not likely. It was nothing special, and the owner didn't advertise in the magazine. The only thing that made the place unique was the patrons. The club was integrated, serving both black and white customers. That made for a nice change. "Maybe."

"You look beautiful tonight." He stared into her eyes.

She wasn't beautiful. At best, she was pretty. "And you're incredibly handsome."

"Beautiful and smart." He leaned forward, and his breath tickled the shell of her ear. "With a discerning eye."

She tamped down opinions that Nick didn't like. She produced sugary smiles when her emotions bubbled like the witches' caldron in *Macbeth*. She ignored the acid at the back of her throat when he looked at other women. *Purely in a professional sense, darling. You know you're the only one for me.* She did it for moments like this. Moments when he looked into her eyes and somehow convinced her they were better together than apart.

"We make the perfect pair." He claimed a kiss in the darkness, and she shivered at the feel of his firm lips on hers.

"What may I get you?" asked a waiter in a white coat.

Nick pulled away from her. "Champagne. Your best bottle."

And, just like that, their moment ended. Why didn't he ask her what she wanted? Not Champagne. Not in a speak like this one. This was the sort of place where one ordered a sealed bottle of White Horse.

Their drinks ordered, Nick returned his attention to her, his fingers grazing her bare knee before taking her hand. "This is nice. Just the two of us." They were unlikely to run into anyone they knew at The Red Door. New York might be a big city, but when everyone frequented the same clubs and parties, it could feel like a small town. It was a rare club where Freddie didn't recognize multiple faces.

"It is nice."

"Moss Hart says the singer is—his words—the cat's pajamas." Nick liked to encourage new talent. There were grateful actors and singers all over the city who swore that Nick had given them their start.

A woman joined the trio in the corner. Enormous brown eyes took up most of her heart-shaped face. The golden-brown shade of her skin was accentuated by the gold beaded dress that clung to her lithe body. She shimmied, and the room quieted. Only then did she open her glossy red lips and sing.

Her voice was whisky and velvet and sex. And Nick gazed at her as if she held the secrets of the universe in her delicate hands.

Freddie could almost see the cogs spinning in his mind. The singer had "it," that combination of sex appeal and talent that drew Nick like a moth to a flame. His tongue rolled out like a red carpet. Well, metaphorically.

Unfortunately, she recognized his expression. She'd last seen it when he encountered a stunning ingenue. There was no question. Nick wanted the singer, and not just on a stage in his latest production.

"Nick!"

He didn't move, didn't register that she'd spoken.

"Nick!"

He remained focused on the singer.

The woman on stage ran her palms down her hips. If Freddie did that, people would think she had sweaty palms. The siren? The move was as sensual and inviting as her voice.

I'll find my man,

I'll make him happy,

Like no other woman can.

She'd endured one bout of infidelity. She wouldn't survive a second.

"Nick!" If she somehow managed to claim his attention, he'd tell her she was being fanciful. And jealous.

Maybe she was jealous. But Nick might do her the courtesy of disguising his interest in other women. Especially when they were together.

"Nick!"

Nothing.

Without another word, she collected her evening bag and rose from the table.

He didn't notice.

She marched out of the little club, hailed a taxi, and asked herself a painful question. *How long would it take for him to notice she was gone?*

A second equally painful question burned in her chest. *Why did she care?*

The phone rang. The jangling sounded like an alarm bell inside her head. With a pitiful groan, Freddie clutched a pillow to her ears. The space behind her eyes throbbed, her mouth felt as if she'd dined on cotton balls, and the sunlight streaming through the windows sliced through her aching brain like a saber. She sealed her eyes shut.

In retrospect, stopping by the Mirador for a drink or three after she left Nick had been a grave mistake.

The phone continued its head-splitting ring.

She fumbled on the bedside table for her watch, barely parted her eyelids, and looked at the time. Her watch had stopped. It couldn't possibly be 2:00 o'clock. With the utmost care, she inched her head to the left until she saw her clock. It read the same.

At least it was the wrong time of day for her mother to call. At 2:00 in the afternoon, she'd be seated at a table in one of her friend's drawing rooms playing bridge or mahjong and gossiping.

What if it was Nick?

With a shaking hand, she reached for the phone. "Hello?"

"Freddie?" Clem's voice boomed across the line. "Are you free this evening?"

"No." She planned on spending the rest of her life in bed.

"Don't be silly. I'm leaving for Paris on Monday. It'll be months before we see each other."

Freddie struggled to sit up. A crystal pitcher and tumbler sat on the table next to the bed. She needed water. "Hold the line, Clem." She poured herself a glass and drank. Nothing had ever tasted better. "I have something of a headache. Can we talk about this later?"

"What did you do last night?"

"I left Nick."

"About time." Her friend had not approved of her latest beau.

"Then I went to the Mirador for a drink."

"Have you eaten?"

"No." Her stomach flip-flopped at the thought of food.

"Make yourself eggs and bacon and hot coffee, then call me back."

"I don't think I could eat."

"Trust me," Clem insisted. "Grease is the answer. I'll talk to you in an hour or so."

The receiver went dead in Freddie's hand.

She dragged herself into the bathroom and stared at the walking corpse in the mirror. Dammit to hell. She should have skipped that last cocktail.

An hour later, she did feel better. The hammering in her brain had subsided to a dull thud, and the queasiness in her stomach had abated. With the aid of a few cups of hot coffee and several glasses of cold water, she'd managed to banish the cotton from her mouth. Yes, she felt better, but she didn't feel good.

The phone rang. Loudly. She picked it up before it rang a second time.

"How do you feel?" asked Clem.

She'd never noticed how her friend brayed until now. "Barely human."

"You sound better. Dinner?"

"With you and John?" The alternative was staying home and moping.

"Yes." A telltale hitch in Clem's voice put Freddie on alert. She could always tell when her friend was hiding something.

"Is someone else joining us?"

"Possibly."

"Who?"

"A buddy of John's. I'll pick you up at eight."

"The last thing I want is another man."

"You're a romantic at heart. You might be heartsick today, but you'll recover and find someone new. Someone better."

"Maybe I'll swear off men."

"Ha! You plan to travel through life alone?"

Freddie grinned. "Don't be silly. I won't be alone. I have you."

"Don't you be silly. I know you better than anyone else in the world. You won't be happy with just me. I'm dizzy and shallow, and I don't read your column."

"You don't read my column?"

"I don't read anything but the society page."

"I'm wounded. I thought you were my biggest fan."

"I am, dear, when it comes to you. You. Not your work. And your biggest fan wants you to be happy."

Freddie glanced in the mirror one last time. She'd chosen a silver Molyneux frock that complemented her eyes. The dress was simple, a satin sheath with a high neckline and no ornamentation. Clem would hate it until she saw the back that plunged to the curve of Freddie's bottom. She touched up her crimson lipstick, draped a silk stole around her shoulders, and picked up her gloves and a beaded evening bag from the console next to the door.

When she stepped off the elevator, Clem's eyes narrowed. "That's your best dress?"

"At least I'm ready on time." She swiveled her feet, and the satin swirled around her calves.

"Go change. I'll wait."

"No." Freddie smiled sweetly at the disapproving look on Clem's face.

"Freddie," Clem insisted, "we're not going to church. You can change your frock. I'll wait. Really, I don't mind a bit." Clem's daring peacock green gown complemented her creamy complexion and blond hair. The skirt was nothing more than strings of beads. Clem's legs would be visible to her thighs when she walked.

"I like this dress," Freddie insisted. Her eyes danced as she allowed one side of her stole to slip off her shoulder. She pirouetted, displaying her bare back to Clem and the doorman.

"Oh. Well, then. Let's go."

She followed Clem to a waiting cab. "Where are we going?"

"Can you believe it? There's not a decent Chinese restaurant in all of France!"

"Imagine that. Whatever will you do?"

"I suppose I'll eat croque madame and croissants and escargot. But tonight, we're eating Chinese. The Bamboo Inn."

She was going back to Harlem. Only a few blocks from The Red Door. Was Bony safe? She could request a small detour, but then she'd have to talk about last night. And she did not want to talk about last night.

When they arrived at the restaurant, she and Clem breezed past dance floor and the less desirable tables and climbed the stairs to the balcony.

John and his friend stood as they approached the table. The

friend was gangly and wore glasses. His tuxedo jacket didn't fit properly, too short in the cuffs, as if he'd borrowed it for the evening. As Freddie watched, he pushed the specs up his nose with his middle finger.

Introductions were made. The friend's name was Silas, and he had a voice that could kindly be called nasal.

Freddie shot Clem a look, and they sat.

An uncomfortable silence settled around them, and Clem tugged at the fingers of her gloves without actually removing them. "Look! Isn't that A'lelia Walker?" She nodded at a woman walking toward their table.

"Who?" Silas looked over his shoulder.

"A'lelia Walker. She's an heiress." Clem's voice dropped to a stage whisper. "You know, the joy goddess of Harlem, denizen of the Dark Tower. Everyone wants an invitation to her parties."

A statuesque black woman in a flamboyant gown sailed past them. Every eye in the room followed her progress, and waiters circled around her like jacks in a game of three-card monte.

"But who is she?" Silas's gaze tracked the woman's progress through the club.

"Her mother developed beauty products. A'lelia runs the company."

The tilt of Silas's narrow head suggested he wasn't impressed. "What's the Dark Tower?"

"That's what people call her salon," Clem explained. "I'd love to be invited."

"It's a literary salon, my darling. You'd have to read more than the society page." Despite his mocking tone, John's hand traveled across the white tablecloth and squeezed Clem's.

"You beast. I read." Clem looked around the table, her eyes rounded with sincerity. "I do! I just finished *The Sheik*."

John did his best to cover a guffaw with a cough.

"I don't believe I'm familiar with that book," said Silas. He looked the sort to read accounting ledgers. For fun.

"It's a wonderful story. So exciting! It's about a girl who doesn't want to get married. She travels to Algeria and insists on going on a trek through the Sahara. A sheik kidnaps her, and they fall madly in love. It's terribly romantic."

"I don't think that's the kind of literature they discuss at the Black Tower," John commented drily.

"Their loss." Clem tossed her blond head. "What are you reading, Silas? Did you know Freddie writes?"

"The new Philo Vance mystery," he replied. "And, no, I didn't know."

Freddie brought the Champagne flute to her lips and let its cold bubbles fill her mouth. She'd have had more fun sitting at home, moping over Nick.

"She's not a novelist like Edith Hull," Clem clarified. "She just writes a column."

"Darling," John scolded, "It's not *just* a column. It's a column in the most successful magazine in the city. And since you can't write so much as a coherent shopping list, perhaps you should eschew the word 'just.'"

"Whatever you do, don't let him get away." Freddie smiled at Clem's escort who had such wonderful taste.

"Don't be ridiculous. He shouldn't let me get away."

Around them, the restaurant bustled. Waiters carrying trays of Chinese food sliced through crowds of people and the haze of cigarette smoke. Titters of sparkling laughter answered charming declarations of questionable sincerity. The mirrored ball which hung above the dance floor spun, casting a moveable rainbow.

John draped a possessive arm around Clem's nearly-naked shoulders. His hand squeezed gently, and Clem's blond hair failed to hide the kiss she swept across his knuckles.

The intimate gesture made Freddie feel like a hungry beggar with her nose pressed against a bakery window, tempted but unable to afford so much as a taste. She turned away from the happy couple and searched for a safe topic. "Do you usually read mysteries, Silas?"

"Honestly, I don't have much time for reading. Too busy at the office."

"What is it you do?"

"I'm an accountant."

She'd been right. He did read ledgers. At least he got paid for it. She swallowed a sigh. It promised to be a long evening. She felt a headache coming on. Soon. A headache that would send her home.

After dinner—bird's nest soup and chicken chow mein—she made her excuses, ignoring the daggers Clem shot with her eyes.

"I'm sorry. Truly, I am. But last night caught up with me. Silas—" she slid out of their booth "—it was a pleasure meeting you. Clem, we'll talk before you sail."

"I'll walk you out." Silas slid out of the booth and latched onto her arm just above her elbow.

The man's touch was unwelcome, and she barely resisted shaking off his fingers. Instead, she offered a tight smile and hurried toward the stairs.

When they emerged from the building, Silas scanned the street. "Wait here. I'll hail us a cab."

Us? No, thank you.

To her left, a handful of people gathered around something on the sidewalk.

Curiosity drew her. Her mother always said that curiosity killed the cat. But Freddie wasn't a cat. Besides, she had a column to fill. Readers loved a hint of danger mixed in with her recommendations on where to find the best dance bands or beef bourguignon. She elbowed past a man in a rusty tux, and her heart rose to her throat. "Bony!"

The boy, who was splayed across the sidewalk, didn't move.

Freddie knelt on the pavement. Why was there blood? So

much blood? Her heart and throat constricted, making it almost impossible to breathe. "Bony."

Bony turned his head toward her.

Thank God. He was alive. She clasped his hand. "Where are you hurt?"

"I'm fine."

The pool of blood said differently.

"Where, Bony?"

His free hand hovered above his ribs.

"How bad?"

"I'll be fine."

She didn't believe him. Not for a second. But she wasn't going to argue the point. "What happened?"

"I got robbed." He winced and pushed onto his elbows.

"Did you get a look at your attacker?"

Bony gave a pained nod. "Red's gonna kill me."

"Who's Red?"

Bony frowned at her as if she'd said something remarkably stupid.

"Your boss?"

His frown deepened. "What will I tell him?"

"Don't worry about Red. I'll make up whatever was stolen. Can you stand?"

Bony pushed higher on his elbows, near to sitting, and then gasped.

"Freddie!" A man's voice claimed her attention.

She glanced over her shoulder and found Silas lurking.

An appalled expression twisted his narrow face. "What are you doing?"

"Helping my friend."

He looked down his long, thin nose. "You know this person?"

"I just said he was my friend. Bony, should I call an ambulance?"

"No!"

"Let me see the wound."

With evident reluctance, the boy peeled back his shirt. The cut across his ribs was long, but it didn't look deep.

"Fine." She ceded. "Let's get you in a taxi. I'll take you home."

"Freddie!" Silas sounded outraged.

"What?" A sharp edge snuck into her voice.

He reached for her hand as if he meant to pull her away from Bony. "You can't be serious."

She was serious as a knife to the chest. "Silas, this is where our acquaintance ends."

He gaped at her, his mouth working like a goldfish in a bowl.

She gave Silas her back and gently helped Bony off the sidewalk, ignoring the way the boy's blood soaked her hem and her gloves. Then, without another glance at John's odious friend, she climbed into the cab he'd hailed and took Bony to his mother.

CHAPTER 3

Freddie sat at Penelope's kitchen table and ached with sadness.

Penelope, a woman who'd always glowed with an inner light, barely flickered. Pain had etched her face. The whites of her eyes had yellowed, and she was even thinner than her son.

When she arrived, Freddie had taken charge. She'd asked Penelope for the name of a doctor who might come and sew up Bony's wound, then sent one of the neighbor children to fetch him. She'd opened the windows and aired out the small apartment. She'd watched over Bony as he fell asleep. She'd made tea. Now, she and Penelope sat with their fingers wrapped around the warm mugs.

Tears gathered in Penelope's eyes. "Thank you for bringing him home. I told him working for Red Garrett was too dangerous."

Together, she and Penelope could get Bony off the streets. "I'll find him a boarding school."

"He won't leave, not while..." Penelope's gaze fell to her lap. *Not while she was dying.* "I want to keep him with me, but I worry what will happen to him when I'm gone. My sister isn't good with children."

"I'll help."

Penelope looked up, and her brows rose. "You?"

"He's a bright boy. He should be in school. He should go to college."

Bony's mother managed a small, wistful smile. "My son in college?"

"Why not? He could be a doctor or a lawyer or a mathematician."

"You're a young woman, Miss Freddie. You don't need to be raising another woman's child."

Freddie waved away her objection. "Bony's the little brother I never had. But we're getting ahead of ourselves. You'll beat this, and he'll stay with you."

"Pretty lies, Miss Freddie. The doctor says six months." She closed her eyes.

Freddie's jaw ached with the need to cry. She swallowed her tears and smiled brightly. Because, when one's heart was breaking, one smiled. That's what everyone did after the war. And Freddie had never stopped smiling. If she didn't have laughter and gaiety and dancing, she'd spend all her time grieving her brother. And not just Grey. So many brothers and fathers and husbands lost. And no way to fill the holes they left behind. Sadness nearly consumed her whenever she thought about it. She reached for Penelope's hand.

Penelope drew her fingers into a fist, avoiding Freddie's touch, as if kindness might undo her. "I'm not afraid of dying. The good Lord will make sure I'm reunited with Bony's father." She tugged at the collar of her dress. "But I'm afraid for my son. He's on a dangerous path. Who cut him?"

"I didn't see. I found Bony on the sidewalk just after it happened. He seemed more worried about his boss than his attacker."

Penelope rubbed a painfully thin hand across her tired eyes. "Red will expect Bony to come up with what was stolen."

"I'll cover it."

"You don't need to do that."

"I want to. Please, let me."

Penelope gave a tiny nod. "I'd rather Bony owe you than Red."

Bony would owe her nothing. "I want Bony to come down to the magazine tomorrow."

"Why?"

"We have a sketch artist." A cartoonist. "Bony can describe his attacker, and Tom will draw him."

"Then what?"

"Then we give the sketch to the police."

Penelope's laugh sounded painful. And dry. Like old leaves. "No police."

Why ever not? "Bony was robbed."

"You think the police will care my boy was robbed? They'll arrest him for running numbers for Red."

"Fine. We'll give the sketch to Red."

"If Red finds him, the man will pay."

"What does that mean?"

Penelope tilted her head as if Freddie had just uttered something nonsensical and utterly naïve.

Oh. Whoever had cut Bony could expect something worse that a stab wound. Perhaps she wouldn't give the sketch to Red.

The expression on Penelope's gaunt face turned cold. "I'll make sure Bony's there."

LIFE WOULD BE DULL WITHOUT FRIENDS. THEY BRING LAUGHTER and fun and unexpected trips to the Bamboo Inn. For those among us who haven't yet been, The Bamboo Inn features

Oriental cuisine, a jazz band, and dancing. You'll spot college lads who know their way around the dance floor holding pretty co-eds, grande dames with their banker husbands, and high Harlem. Try for a booth on the balcony where the lights reflected from the mirror ball color one's chow mein indigo or rose.

A tap on the door had Freddie lifting her fingers from her typewriter's keys. "Come in."

Annie, her assistant, stepped into the office. "There's a young man here to see you. He says his name is Bony and that you're expecting him."

"I am."

"You have a column due by three." She meant that Freddie didn't have time to entertain a child from Harlem.

"The column is nearly done. Please, show Bony in. Also, a plate of cookies and lemonade wouldn't be amiss."

Annie's lips flattened, but she nodded.

"And we'll need Tom."

"Tom Shaw?"

"Yes." She'd forgotten to mention Bony's possible arrival to Annie, but she'd ridden up on the elevator with Tom, and he'd agreed to help with a drawing.

When Bony entered her office, he wasn't alone. A second boy, almost as thin as Bony, trailed behind him. "Good morning, Miss Freddie."

"Good morning. How are you feeling? How's your mother?"

He flashed her his sweet smile. "Better." Then he nodded toward his friend. "This here is Dabb."

"Nice to meet you, Dabb." She extended her hand.

The boy, who looked to be all of twelve, wiped his palm against his pants, and then gave her fingers a quick shake.

"Dabb is covering for me a few days while I take Mama down to Baltimore."

"Baltimore?"

"Her sister lives there." He jammed his hands in his pockets.

"My friend Jojo was robbed last night. Cut, too." Bony rubbed the wound on his torso. "It's got everyone scared. Dabb's worried about taking over my blocks. If your friend can make a likeness, Dabb'll know who to watch out for, who to avoid." It was a clever idea, and it might keep Dabb safe.

"Please, sit down."

The boys sat on the other side of her desk and looked around her office. It wasn't overly large. Just big enough for her desk, two chairs, and a divan where she sometimes napped. The walls were painted cream and crowded with art, framed illustrations by Mary Wilson Preston, a Florine Stettheimer oil, and a Charles Demuth watercolor. Two windows allowed for natural light, and pots of Swedish ivy, kept alive by Annie, rested on the sills. Her desk was wooden and utilitarian, its surface covered by a type-writer and a pair of wire bins—one for completed work, the other for pieces that had been returned to her with edits. Today, there were also two dozen red roses in a crystal vase and a card, written by a florist, that said, "Please, forgive me. I love you. Nick."

"This is nice," said Bony.

"I like it."

"Should I tell you about the man who robbed me?"

"Let's wait till Tom arrives."

"Freddie?" Tom stuck his head through the doorway.

"Oh, good. You're here. Tom, this is Bony. Bony meet Tom Shaw. He's an artist. And Dabb. Meet Dabb."

Tom, who carried a sketchbook and a fistful of charcoal pencils, perched on the edge of her desk.

Annie followed him. She centered a plate of cookies and a pitcher of milk in front of the two boys. "There's no lemonade. I'll be back with glasses."

Dabb's eyes rounded, and he wiped his hands on his pants a second time. "Those are for us?"

"Yes. And Tom."

Tom opened his sketchbook to a blank page. "Tell me about the man's face, Bony. Was it round or oval or square?"

"Square, but long."

Tom began his drawing, asking questions, erasing lines when Bony said the eyes were too close together.

Annie breezed in with a tray of glasses and poured the milk.

Dabb attacked the cookie plate. Washing down the shortbread with cold milk.

Freddie turned the florist's card in her fingers.

Forty-five minutes later, Tom had produced a drawing of a man with an off-center nose, mean eyes, and a scar on the left side of his face that ran from his hairline to his square jaw.

"That's him," said Bony.

Dabb studied the drawing, committing the face to memory.

Freddie did the same. "Thanks, Tom."

He tore out the page and handed it to her. "I need to get back to work, but I'll look forward to that bottle."

She'd promised him real scotch.

"It will be on your desk in the morning."

When Tom opened the office door, Annie stuck her head in, annoyance writ large across her pretty features. "Nick Peters has called three times. He's on the line again, and he won't take 'no' for an answer."

Freddie sighed. "Give me a minute, then I'll talk to him." She turned to Bony. "When do you leave for Baltimore?"

"Tomorrow. Tonight, I'm showing Dabb the ropes."

She nodded. "Give your mother my love."

He glanced at the sketch in her hand. "What will you do with that?"

She wasn't sure. She'd promised not to go to the police, but she didn't fancy Red Garrett's version of justice. "I don't know."

He nodded as if he understood her dilemma, and then he grabbed Dabb by the elbow and hauled the younger boy toward the door.

Dabb dragged his heels, his gaze fixed on the last cookie. "You gonna eat that?"

Bony gave an outraged gasp as if he couldn't quite believe his friend's impudence.

Freddie held out the plate. "Please take it. You'd be doing me a favor."

Dabb wasted no time snatching the last cookie. Then he grinned up at her with adoration dancing in his brown eyes. "These cookies sure are good. Thank you."

"You're welcome. Bony—" she held out a card with her home and office phone numbers on it "—if you or your mother need anything—*anything*—you call me."

"I will. Thank you, Miss Freddie."

She nodded. Slowly. "Don't take any wooden nickels."

Bony flashed her his sweet smile. Then the boys scampered off, leaving her to deal with Nick.

CHAPTER 4

This was a mistake.

She should have found a spine.

Or pride.

Or self-respect.

Or a harder heart.

Or just the ability to turn Nick down.

Instead, she'd found herself giving in.

True, Nick had wooed her with seductive promises.

She was his everything.

He couldn't live without her.

He'd do anything if she forgave him.

He loved her.

Pretty words that had landed her at a table with Nick at the Tsarina's Closet.

Ever since the White Army's loss to the Bolsheviks, Russian émigrés had been arriving in New York in droves. Many of them claimed aristocratic titles; a few were telling the truth. Regardless, clubs celebrating Imperial Russia popped up faster than dandelions in the spring. At this one, the waiters wore Cossack-style vests and ushankas.

The club's air was redolent with smoke and vodka and jazz, and soft amber lights from crystal chandeliers revealed golden double-headed eagle wallpaper. A red velvet curtain embroidered with gold sickles hid the entrance to the card room. And a dark mahogany bar, stretching the length of the back wall, was stocked with more vodka than Freddie had ever seen.

"I'm so sorry about the other night." Nick reached across the table and clasped her hand. "Thank you for coming out with me. I never meant to ignore you."

"We need to talk." And not at a club. No, they needed a long, real talk about what they each wanted, because their current arrangement was putting too much strain on her emotions. It was affecting her work. "I don't mind a bit of drama, but we can't keep this up."

His brows lifted. "Drama?"

"If I'm with a man, I need to be able to trust him."

"I've told you, you can trust me."

"And you've shown me, I can't."

"Freddie, don't be so…"

"Dramatic?" She freed her hand. "This will never work."

"Don't say that. I love you. I'll do better. Be better."

Despite their problems, her heart encouraged her to believe him. When things were good between them, they were very, very good. "I don't know, Nick."

"Freddie, don't say that." He gazed into her eyes. "You know you're the only one for me."

"Nickie!" A bottle blonde in a wisp of a dress leaned over Nickie's back and snaked her arms around his neck.

He attempted to extricate himself from the human python. "Let go, Dorcas."

The woman's face crumpled. "But Nickie—"

"Let. Go. Now."

Dorcas dropped her arms and shot Freddie a venomous glare. "Who are you?"

Freddie felt her brows lift. "Who are you?" If Nick's gaze lingered on the strange woman for more than an instant, they were finished.

Nick shifted in his chair, suddenly uncomfortable. But rather than send the tomato packing, he lifted his glass to his lips and drank deeply. "Sweetheart, this is—"

"I'm Nickie's fiancée." Dorcas planted a lingering kiss on his jaw.

Nick choked on his drink. "Dorcas, no."

Freddie felt frozen in place, too horrified to move.

The woman smoothed a lock of Nick's hair into place. "After last night, of course, we'll be married."

The color drained from Nick's face. "Dorcas—"

Freddie suspected she'd turned as pale as Nick. His pretty promises had been lies. Each and every one.

"Freddie, she's lying. I wasn't with her last night."

She didn't believe him. She gathered her evening bag and wrap and stood, nearly knocking over her chair in her haste.

"Wait." Dorcas held up her hands. "You're Freddie? Dammit to hell, Nick. Why didn't you tell me? I apologize."

Freddie's lips twisted into a snarl, and she stepped away from the table.

Nick lunged and caught her arm. "Please. Don't go. Listen."

"I'm so sorry, Nick." Dorcas actually sounded contrite. "Freddie, Nick and I have an arrangement."

Freddie snorted. An arrangement. Is that what they were calling sex these days?

"We did not spend last night together. Or any night." Dorcas wrinkled her nose, as if the thought of Nick in her bed was distasteful. "And we never will."

"Then why say you did?"

"I thought you were another hopeful ingenue."

Freddie gawped at her. "I don't understand."

"Nick and I watch out for each other. The man can't enter a

club without being swarmed by aspiring actresses. I chase them off."

"What does Nick do for you?"

"I attract the wrong kind of man. Nick got me out of a jam."

Be that as it may, Freddie's poor heart couldn't take any more. She tugged against Nick's hold on her arm.

He refused to release her. "She's telling the truth."

Maybe she was, but the ups and downs were too much. Freddie was tired of her emotions pulled taut. Tired of drama. "I'm done, Nick."

"Freddie," he pleaded.

"Wait," said Dorcas. "Please, wait. Let me explain. I was with one of Nick's friends."

Nick grimaced.

"One of Nick's former friends. He hit me. Often. He told me he'd kill me if I left him. One night, Nick heard him say just that. Nick got me out. He invested in my beauty salon." Dorcas patted her Marcelled hair, and her expression softened. "He saved my life."

Nick might thoughtlessly hurt her feelings, but he could also be kind. Dorcas was proof of that. "I'm glad he helped you. Truly, I am. But I need a break. I'm going home."

She pulled her arm free, caught her heel, and stumbled, twisting her ankle and tipping sideways.

Nick leaped forward, catching her before she fell. "Freddie?"

She stared past him, their drama momentarily forgotten. "That's him."

"Who?" Nick demanded.

She regained her footing and jerked her chin toward the bar. "The fellow who robbed Bony."

"Someone robbed the boy from Harlem?" Nick was usually quicker on the uptake.

"Yes." She nodded. "The man at the bar."

He followed her gaze to the man in the chalk-stripe suit. "How could you possibly know that's him?"

"The scar on his face." Just as Bony had described, a ropy scar cut through the man's right eyebrow and down his cheek, ending at his jaw line. "I have a drawing at the office." Not that she needed to explain herself to Nick. She took a step toward the bar.

"Where are you going?" he demanded. "Don't tell me the bar. The man is obviously dangerous."

It was as if Nick didn't know her at all.

Perhaps her glare telegraphed her feelings because he winced. "What do you propose?"

"I'll go to the bar and get his name." It was a solid plan.

"Then what?"

"Then I'll report him to the police." If the gander could lie, so could the goose.

"How will you get his name?"

She shrugged off her wrap and donned an alluring smile. "I'll ask him for it."

Again, he grabbed her arm. "Freddie, don't you dare."

"He's right," said Dorcas. "It'll never work."

"Oh?" Freddie's tone was frosty. She might not be brassy and beautiful, but most men found her passably attractive. She'd get the man's name.

Dorcas shook her head. "Man like that? He's lived rough. He won't believe a high-class woman is chatting him up. But, me? He's exactly my type. Let me do it."

Without giving Freddie a chance to reply, Dorcas walked toward the man who'd raked a knife across Bony's chest.

Freddie moved to follow, but Nick still held her arm. Tightly.

"If you ever want to see me again, you'll let me go."

Slowly his fingers loosened, and his hand dropped. "Please. Be careful." His lips were thin, nearly bloodless. "I meant what I said. I love you."

Without replying, she hurried after Dorcas. The woman sashayed, her hips swayed with the music, and she pretended a level of intoxication that far too many men took as an invitation. She reached the bar and deliberately bumped into the man. "I'm sorry. I don't know how I missed seeing such a big, strong man."

Heavens to Betsy, Dorcas was laying it on thick. Freddie stood near her back, unable to see her face, but she was willing to bet Nick's friend was batting her lashes like mad.

The man didn't seem to mind having a pretty girl bump into him. His eyes lit with interest. "That's okay, doll. Buy you a drink?" With money he stole from children.

"Yes, please. I'm Dorcas."

"Joe."

"What's your last name, Joe?"

"Why do you ask?"

"I like to know who I'm drinking with."

"Smith."

Dorcas stepped away. Went so far as to turn her back on him. Her eyes narrowed when she spotted Freddie lurking a few feet away.

"Don't be like that." Joe's hand landed on Dorcas's shoulder.

A triumphant smile flitted across Dorcas's lips. Then she twisted to face him. "What kind of man lies to a woman before they've even had a drink together?"

He chuckled as if she'd made a good point. "Monteleone. My name's Joe Monteleone."

"That's a good name. More interesting than Smith. You're from New York?"

"Born on Mulberry Street. Moved uptown a few years ago. You?"

"I live in the Village."

"You an artist?"

"An actress."

Joe's eyes sparked with interest. "What are you drinking?"

"What else? Vodka."

Joe waved down the bartender.

"What'll it be, Joe?" asked the bartender.

"A shot of vodka and a scotch."

"Do you come here often?" asked Dorcas.

"You're a nosey broad."

Dorcas shrugged her nearly bare shoulders. "The bartender knows you."

Joe pursed his lips before nodding. "My buddy Dimitri manages the place. I come here most nights."

Freddie faded into the crowd. She had what she needed. A name. Joe Monteleone. And she knew where to find him. Now what?

CHAPTER 5

Freddie stared at her typewriter. Glared, really. What was there to be said about spring hats that hadn't been said a thousand times before? They were straw. They were bedecked with flowers. They were…what the hell were they?

Her brain was too filled with images of Joe Monteleone and his frightening scar. That, and Nick and his goodnight kiss. One she should not have allowed.

She brought her coffee cup to her lips and found it empty. Dammit it to hell, how had that happened?

Tap, tap.

"Come in." Grateful for the interruption, she leaned back in her chair.

Annie stuck her head inside the office. "Your friend Bony is back."

Bony was supposed to be on his way to Baltimore. Freddie rose from her desk. "Show him in."

Annie answered with a small nod. "Of course." Then she eased the door shut.

Why was Bony here? Had Penelope taken a turn for the

worse? Worry twisted Freddie's stomach into a pretzel, and she met him at the door.

His usual smile had disappeared, replaced by a wounded, hang-dog expression that pulled at Freddie's heart. She opened her arms, and he rushed into her embrace.

She held Bony as he shook. It took a few seconds for her to realize he was crying. She wasn't accustomed to comforting children. She didn't know what to do.

She caught Annie's eye over the boy's shoulder, and her secretary made a sympathetic face before easing out of the office.

"Shh." Freddie rubbed a gentle circle on Bony's back. "Shh."

He pulled away from her, wiping his eyes with the back of his hand.

"What's happened?" She took his hand and led him to a chair. "You can tell me."

Bony sank onto the chair as if his skinny legs no longer had the strength to keep him upright. He clasped his hands in his lap and studied his knuckles. "Dabb…"

She crouched next to him and waited, not so patiently, for more.

Bony buried his face in his palms. "He got robbed last night. He's dead."

"Oh, Bony." Freddie sat back on her heels. The boy with a taste for cookies was dead? How could that be? She remembered the glint in his brown eyes. His interest in Tom's sketch. There had to be some mistake. "What happened?"

"I was standing a few feet away, talking to one of my regulars about the races at Belmont Park. Dabb took a bet from Miss Mabel. She always bets the same numbers. Always a nickel bet." He shook his head—an annoyed shake, as if Miss Mabel and her bet were irrelevant. "A man marched up to Dabb and demanded money. Dabb looked at me and froze." Bony wiped his nose with the back of his hand. "I told him to give up the money. I guess the man thought Dabb wasn't fast enough. The man grabbed his shoulder and shook him. Hard enough to rattle his teeth. Dabb dropped the money on the sidewalk, and the man stabbed him in the chest. It was the same man, Miss Freddie. The one who cut me."

A child. Joe Monteleone had murdered a child for a fistful of dollars. The coffee in Freddie's stomach soured.

Bony stared sightlessly at the windows. "There was so much blood."

Freddie wrapped the boy in her arms. "What time did this happen?"

He loosed a small sob. "Eight o'clock."

An hour before she and Nick arrived at The Tsarina's Closet, Joe Monteleone had committed murder. Then he'd gone out for a drink.

"When do you leave for Baltimore?" She wanted Bony to be safe.

"We aren't going. With Dabb gone, Red won't spare me. Mama and I can't go till he finds someone new."

Joe Monteleone had already wounded Bony. He'd killed Dabb. Being on the street was too dangerous. "Bony, working for Red is no life for you."

"What else am I going to do?"

"Go to school. Get an education."

He rolled his eyes. "Who'll put food on the table while I'm sitting in a classroom?"

"I will."

"And Mama?"

"I'll take care of her, too."

His face creased into an expression that was far too cynical and knowing for his years. "You know Mama. She won't take charity."

She might if it got her son off the streets. "Bony, you're smart. You're meant for better things than running numbers."

He shook his head.

"Do you want to end up like Dabb? What would your mother do then?" Guilt. A useful tool in her mother's arsenal. One she'd sworn she'd never use. Look at her now. Wielding guilt like a billy club. But the circumstances were dire. Bony was in danger. And he wasn't listening. "She needs you. She loves you. Losing you would…"

Bony stared at the floor. He didn't have an answer.

She reached for her hat, straw with silk violets at the brim. "Come with me."

"Where are we going?"

"To see your mother." She'd talk sense into both of them if it was the last thing she did.

CHAPTER 6

"You want me to wait?" asked the cabbie.

Freddie clutched her handbag and gathered her courage. "Yes, please. I don't expect to be long." She took a deep breath and immediately regretted it.

In her neighborhood, the warm spring breeze brought the scents of spring flowers, ladies' perfume, men's pomade, and money.

The air that pushed through the taxi's open window smelled of automobile exhaust and other less pleasant things.

The taxi driver turned and looked at her. "Nice girl like you shouldn't be here alone."

She didn't argue. Instead, she steeled her spine, opened the door to the taxi, and stepped onto the cracked sidewalk.

Two men flanked the entrance to her destination, a brick building that had seen better days. Beefy arms crossed over barrel chests, and fearsome scowls seemed to have taken up permanent residence on the men's faces.

She ventured toward them, donning what she hoped was a don't-shoot-me-on-sight smile. "I'm here to see Red Garrett."

The one on the left, who had caterpillars for eyebrows, deepened his scowl. "Who are you?"

"My name is Freddie. I'm a friend of Bony Johnson."

Neither man moved. Not so much as a muscle.

She drew a steadying breath and remembered what Penelope had told her to say. "Someone has been robbing Mr. Garrett's boys. At knife point. Taking Mr. Garrett's money. Hurting the boys. I have a name for him."

"You?" Caterpillar's disbelief was evident.

"Me. Also, I know where Mr. Garrett can find the man."

The two men exchanged a glance, and then Caterpillar stepped inside.

"You wait here," said the other.

"Of course."

She waited. Minutes passed. She studied the street. A cobbler. A laundry. A soda fountain. All with bars across their windows. She glanced at the waiting taxi. The cabbie looked nervous. Almost as nervous as she was.

Two men emerged from the building. Caterpillar and a smaller man, who wore a red shirt. Freddie idly wondered if red was his signature color. If that was how he'd gotten his name. Because the man in front of her was definitely the boss. He swaggered. And she could sense power rising off him like the morning mist from the East River.

He studied her for long seconds, and she resisted the urge to fidget. Instead, she lifted her chin and met his dark gaze.

"Who are you?" he demanded.

"Freddie."

He lifted an unamused brow.

"Freddie Archer."

"You know who's been robbing my boys?"

"I do."

"How?"

She reached into her handbag and took out the cartoonist's

sketch, offering it to the intimidating man. "His name is Joe Monteleone."

He took the picture, studying the face. "Ugly mug. How did you get this?"

"I paired Bony and an artist. This is what they came up with. It's a good likeness."

Red gave her a sharp look before returning his gaze to the drawing. "You've actually met him?"

She nodded and wished for a glass of water. Her mouth was dry as dust. "He frequents The Tsarina's Closet. He's friends with the manager, Dimitri."

"Why are you telling me this?"

"I thought you might want to know. He is stealing from you."

He nodded. Slowly. "Woman like you…" His contemptuous expression said he'd judged her and found her lacking "Why not go to the police?"

"I promised Penelope Johnson I wouldn't."

The man's stare bored into her, and she just stopped herself from biting her lower lip. Instead, she tightened her hold on her handbag. She was bringing him information. Good information. He had no reason to toss her in the Hudson.

"If this information pans out, I owe you a favor."

She gave a tiny nod. This. Right here. Right now. It was where everything could go terribly wrong. Please, please, let her voice be steady. "If you find Monteleone, then Bony doesn't work for you anymore."

A tiny smile ghosted Red's lips, so quickly she almost missed it. "What's your interest in Bony?"

"His mother helped raise me. The boy is smart. He should be in school."

"You think he's too good for this life?"

This life. Running numbers. Crime. It was a dangerous question.

"Mr. Garrett—"

"Red."

"Mr. Red—"

"Just Red." The way one corner of his upper lip curled chilled her blood. "No *mister*."

"Red, you seem like a nice man—"

Red snorted.

Perhaps "nice" was a step too far. Red was not a nice man. Anyone could see that. But she would not step backward. She would not retreat. "The children who work for you are getting hurt. I know that must concern you. I'd like to keep Bony safe."

He stared at her for so long that the butterflies in her stomach had time to mount an all-out assault on her nervous system. Finally, when Freddie was ready to crack, he said, "Fine."

"Fine?" she squeaked. Could it be this easy?

"Your tip checks out, then Bony doesn't work for me anymore." The man grunted and then rubbed a hand across his chin. "This neighborhood isn't for you, Freddie Archer. Go home." She'd been dismissed. Red turned his back on her and disappeared into the brick building.

When she didn't move, Caterpillar scowled at her. "That means scram."

She didn't need telling twice. Freddie retreated to her taxi.

"You okay, miss?"

"Fine, thank you." She'd done it. She'd told Red about Joe Monteleone and freed Bony from Red's employ.

"Where to?"

She gave the cabbie the address of a speakeasy on 52nd. After this trip to Harlem, she needed a drink. Or two. Or quite possibly three. How many drinks to wash away signing a man's death warrant? She aimed to find out.

CHAPTER 7

They sat across from each other. The white cloth on the table was pristine. Votive candles cast a golden light. A vase of hyacinths perfumed the air. Champagne bubbled in their glasses. And neither she nor Nick had a single thing to say.

Freddie took a quick sip of wine, wetting her dry throat. "We need to talk."

Nick's gaze caught hers, and he nodded.

"I…" She didn't know how to tell him all the things he should know. "I—"

"Let me go first."

It was her turn to nod. A grateful nod.

"I love you, Freddie. We're good together."

Sometimes.

"We belong together." He tugged at his collar.

Maybe. Or maybe they were so entranced by the good moments that they failed to enumerate the bad ones.

"We've never talked about the future…"

Was he sweating? A bead of perspiration trickled from Nick's temple to his jaw line.

"But I've thought about it. A great deal."

"What about it?" she asked. When she'd thought about the future with Nick, she imagined lazy Sunday mornings spent reading the paper, drinking coffee, and falling back into bed. She imagined a faith and certainty in him that she didn't currently possess.

He reached under the table and pulled out a box. "Please, make me the happiest man on earth. Say you'll be my wife." Nick didn't look happy. He looked green, as if he might upchuck his Champagne at any second. With a sickly smile, he opened the box.

Freddie gasped at the ring. It was enormous with a diamond the size of a martini olive set in white gold. "Nick." She pressed her fingers to her lips. The ring was so very Nick—ridiculously generous.

"That's not a *yes*."

Good Lord, that diamond.

Somehow, she tore her gaze away from the rock and focused on Nick's face. "You promise to be faithful?"

He gazed into her eyes. Deeply. Sincerely. "To my dying day."

God help her, she believed him. "You'll listen to my opinions?"

"On everything."

"You love me?"

"With every fiber of my being."

Her heart beat so hard it was a wonder it remained in her chest. "Then, yes. I'll marry you."

He claimed her hand and slipped the ring onto her finger. Then, he held up her hand and admired the sparkle in the candlelight. "Our lives will be fabulous, Freddie. You'll see. You'll never want for anything. I promise."

"What I want is a partner."

"You have one, my love."

The waiter arrived with their meals.

When he left, Nick picked up his fork. "I found us a house in Connecticut."

A house? "Connecticut?"

"You'll adore it. Five acres. Six bedrooms."

Six bedrooms? "Why Connecticut? Why can't we live in my apartment?" The location was perfect, and the apartment was more than big enough for the two of them.

"Children need fresh air and sunshine, room to run."

"We don't have children."

"But we will."

"And when we do, we can talk about Connecticut."

"This house is too perfect to miss."

"I don't want to commute."

He frowned at her. "Commute?"

"Yes, Nick. Commute. To *Gotham*."

"When we're married, you won't work."

"I want to work."

"Don't be silly, darling."

She'd ignored, sometimes successfully, sometimes less so, Nick's wandering eye. She'd forgiven the way he sometimes seemed to forget her. She'd spent countless hours worrying about Nick, stewing over Nick, dreaming about Nick. Never, not once, had it occurred to her that Nick would ask her to give up her job. "But…"

"I know! You can write from home, like a novelist."

Except she wasn't a novelist. She was a columnist. One who wrote about New York. Not Connecticut.

"Or stories." He pointed his fork at her. "You can write stories like your friend Dorothy Parker."

"I like working for the magazine. It brings me joy."

"So will children."

She stared at the man across the table, a man so wrapped up in his own dreams that hers weren't important. She'd spent a year with him, and he didn't understand the first thing about her. Her job meant the world to her, and he was suggesting that she give it up as if it meant nothing.

"I'm keeping my job, Nick. And I don't want to commute from Connecticut."

"If it makes you feel better, we'll keep your apartment. I can use it when I need to stay in the city."

"I'm not quitting my job, Nick."

"Freddie, be reasonable. You can't possibly love that job more than you love me."

She was the one being unreasonable? "What would you say if I told you to give up producing on Broadway? What if I insisted you move to the country?"

"I'm not suggesting Iowa."

"You might as well be."

"So dramatic. You'll see. You'll love the house. And the fresh air. It's marvelous." He frowned at her untouched plate. "You're not eating your dinner."

"I'm not very hungry." She tugged at the ring.

"Too loose?" he asked.

Too tight.

This was their last night together. Nick might be imagining a beginning, but she knew better. They might love each other, but he didn't listen to her. He wanted more than she could give. Tonight was a goodbye. In the morning, they'd go their separate ways. "It's a beautiful ring, Nick."

He beamed. "I knew you'd like it."

She held out her hand and admired the diamond. Too bad she couldn't keep it.

CHAPTER 8

Freddie walked into Penn Station with Bony and Penelope at her side. Each step forward felt like slogging through heavy snow. Why didn't she feel light? Or free? There was no man to weigh her down.

As usual, the station's lobby was crowded with travelers.

Bony tilted his head and gasped, a common reaction the first time one entered the station. The ceilings soared nearly a hundred-and-fifty feet high, and the marble columns and floors were reminiscent of the Roman baths at Caracalla. Not that she'd been to Caracalla, but that was what the Pennsylvania Railroad claimed, and she didn't doubt them.

"This way." She pointed toward the glass and steel canopy that led down to the tracks. Rays of early morning sun shone through the glass, illuminating the stairs.

Penelope remained rooted. "Thank you, Miss Freddie. For everything."

"My pleasure."

Gratitude filled Penelope's brown eyes, threatening to spill over. "What you've done…"

Freddie's stomach lurched. What she'd done. She'd heard

through the gossip-laden grapevine that a man with a scar on his face had been escorted out of The Tsarina's Closet. Kicking and screaming. She carried the responsibility for that. She pulled a dime from her handbag and held it out. "Bony, what's your favorite candy?"

"Either Oh Henry! or Charleston Chew."

"Why don't you buy a treat for the train ride?" She nodded toward a newsstand.

Bony didn't need telling twice. He plucked the coin from her fingers and dashed to the stand.

When he was out of earshot, Freddie faced Penelope and asked, "What happened to Monteleone?" She'd told herself that ignorance was bliss. That she'd be better off not knowing. But her conscience wouldn't allow it. She had to know.

Penelope's thin face drew into a grimace. "You sure you want to know?"

Was she? No. "Yes."

"He won't be knifing any more children."

"Oh." The air left Freddie's lungs, and she pressed her palm against the sudden ache in her chest.

"Red's boys broke his kneecaps." A small smile lit Penelope's features. "With a lead pipe."

Maimed, not murdered. Freddie breathed a sigh of relief.

Penelope stared at her as if she were a mystery to be solved. "You told Red about Monteleone. You had to know they might kill him."

"That doesn't mean I wanted his death as a black mark on my soul." She'd made a promise to a dying woman, and she'd kept it. She hadn't gone to the police. And she was grateful beyond measure that keeping her promise hadn't killed a man.

"Monteleone will never walk again." Penelope's gaze found her son. "It's more justice than the police would have offered."

Freddie wasn't about to argue. She reached into her handbag, withdrew an envelope, and offered it to Penelope.

Penelope frowned as if Freddie were holding the lead pipe that Red's thugs had used on Monteleone. "What's this?"

"Information about Bony's new school in Baltimore. He's enrolled in the summer session. The tuition is paid. They'll bill me for the autumn semester."

"I can't—"

"You can. He's your son."

"But—"

"No *buts*. You and your sister make sure he actually attends."

Penelope accepted the envelope.

Bony, whose pockets bulged with not one, but two candy bars, rejoined them as his mother slipped the envelope into her handbag. "Thank you for the candy, Miss Freddie."

"You're welcome. Now, come along. You don't want to miss your train." She wanted Bony out of New York. A bargain was a bargain, and she doubted Red would renege, but she wouldn't rest easy until Bony was in Maryland.

They descended to the tracks. Slowly. Since Bony insisted on carrying both his and his mother's suitcases. When they reached the platform, he dropped the cases, flexing and curling his fingers.

"Bony?"

He glanced her way.

"Will you make me a promise?"

He nodded immediately. "Anything you want, Miss Freddie."

"Promise me you'll attend school."

He stared at her as if she'd asked for the moon.

"You said anything I wanted. That's what I want. I want you to attend school and do your best and make your mama proud."

The sweet smile lightened his face. "I promise, Miss Freddie."

She hugged him, blinking back tears. "Do you still have my phone numbers?"

"I do."

"You keep those and call me whenever you need me."

A conductor with a voice like a bull horn bellowed, "All aboard!"

Bony pulled away from her, reclaiming the two suitcases and lugging them up the first step onto the train.

"Goodbye, Penelope." Freddie's jaw ached with unshed tears. She doubted they would see each other again.

"You're a good woman, Miss Freddie. I'm proud to know you."

Good? Her actions had robbed a man of his ability to walk.

"Monteleone knifed Bony. He killed Dabb. He wouldn't have stopped. Not ever. He would have killed more children." It was as if Penelope could read her mind and knew how to assuage her guilt. "You have good instincts, Miss Freddie. You did the hard thing, but it was also the right thing."

"How—"

"I've known you since you were knee high to a grasshopper. You think I can't tell what you're thinking? Just like I can tell there's something else bothering you."

"This morning—" Freddie pressed a palm to her chest where it felt as if her heart was shattering "—I did the hard thing. I'm hoping it was the right thing."

"Like I said, your instincts are good." Penelope took her hands and squeezed them with surprising strength. "Believe in yourself. I do."

Freddie swallowed a fresh wave of tears. "I'll miss you."

"I'll miss you, too. And when I join the good Lord, I'll keep an eye on you."

"I'll be fine. Keep an eye on Bony instead."

Slowly, painfully, Penelope hauled herself onto the train. "Like I said, I can tell what you're thinking, and I reckon you'll be the one watching Bony. Thank you for that, Miss Freddie. You're giving my boy a future."

Freddie stood on the platform as the train pulled out of the station.

When the caboose disappeared, she adjusted the brim of her hat, straw with silk violets and a grosgrain band. She felt not light, but better. The sun was shining. Boys in Harlem were a bit safer. And she had a column to write.

FREDDIE HAS HER OWN NEWSLETTER! SIGN UP HERE:
https://www.juliemulhernauthor.com/freddie-newsletter

PRE-ORDER MURDER IN MANHATTAN HERE:
https://www.hachettebookgroup.com/titles/julie-mulhern/murder-in-manhattan/9781538773567/

THANK YOU!

Thank you for spending time with Freddie. She is inspired by Lois Long, the columnist who wrote as Lipstick for *The New Yorker* in the 1920s.

I don't remember how I discovered Lois, but I do remember falling in love with her writing. She was funny and arch and utterly entertaining.

I wanted to travel back in time and join her for a gin rickey at one of the speakeasies she frequented. I wanted to stroll Fifth Avenue with her as she gave her opinions on the latest fashions in the windows. I wanted to join her table at The Cotton Club as she listened to her favorite musician, Duke Ellington.

Time machines being sparse, the only way I could hang out with Lois was to base a character on her. I had a ball writing about her, and I like to think that Lois, who was always up for fresh fun, would approve.

You can pre-order Freddie's first mystery, **Murder in Manhattan**, here:

https://www.hachettebookgroup.com/titles/julie-mulhern/murder-in-manhattan/9781538773567/

The Country Club Murders

The Deep End

Guaranteed to Bleed

Clouds in My Coffee

Send in the Clowns

Watching the Detectives

Cold as Ice

Shadow Dancing

Back Stabbers

Telephone Line

Stayin' Alive

Killer Queen

Night Moves

Lyin' Eyes

Big Shot

Fire and Rain

Killing Me Softly

Back in Black

Tight Rope

Bad Blood

Rich Girl

ALSO BY JULIE MULHERN

Freddie Archer Series

Murder by Moonlight (prequel novella)

Murder in Manhattan

The Poppy Fields Adventures

Fields' Guide to Abduction

Fields' Guide to Assassins

Fields' Guide to Voodoo

Fields' Guide to Fog

Fields' Guide to Pharaohs

Fields' Guide to Dirty Money

Fields' Guide to Smuggling

Fields' Guide to Secrets